# Seattle Blues

# Dedication

For Ruby, Dagmar, and Aletha,
the grandmothers in my life

# Seattle Blues

**Michael Wenberg**

Published by WestSide Books
60 Industrial Road
Lodi, NJ 07644
973-458-0485
Fax: 973-458-5289

Library of Congress Control Number: 2008911811


International Standard Book Number: 978-1-934813-04-1
Cover illustration Copyright © by Lori McElrath-Eslick
Cover design by David Lemanowicz
Interior design by Chinedum Chukwu

Printed in the United States of America
10 9 8 7 6 5 4 3 2 1

First Edition

# Seattle Blues

# Chapter One

"It's for the best, Maya!"

Those infamous last words followed me up the steps of the Greyhound bus, nagging me like an out-of-tune song you can't get out of your head.

*It's for the best? Who's Mom kidding? Last time I checked, I was the one being sent away—to the last place on earth I want to go.*

I hesitated at the top of the steps, tempted by the chance, however slight, that pleading my case one last time might make a difference.

But the bus driver put an end to it. I suppose he was taking orders directly from my mom.

"Best find a seat, miss," he said, as he pulled on a big metal handle, closing the door tight. "It's not like shopping for shoes. One seat's pretty much like the others."

Any other day, I would have said something sassy in response. But not that morning. I felt the bus shudder through the soles of my sneakers, then heard it hiss as the driver released the brakes. A glance over his shoulder told me my time was up. I choked back an angry scream of frustration and flopped into the pair of empty seats directly behind him. What else could I do?

As I shrugged out of my backpack, I glanced out the window. There was my mom, walking along beside the bus, close enough to reach out and touch the glass. She looked so sad to see me go.

But I knew better. I knew she was glad to get rid of me.

The bus belched one final time, turned out onto the street and picked up speed. I was startled to see Mom break into a graceful run, easily keeping pace with the bus. I tapped the window with my fingers, my heart fluttering with sudden hope. Maybe she was having second thoughts?

I imagined her transformed into a superwoman, not bothering to yell for the bus driver to halt, but jumping in front, grabbing the bumper, and *forcing* that bus to stop, sneakers smoking from the friction. Then she'd bolt around to the side, tear open the door, and say, "Come on, Maya. Grab your bag. I've changed my mind." And I'd be so happy.

But when I blinked a moment later, she was no longer right outside my window. I turned around quickly and spotted her, standing alone behind us, growing smaller as we sped away. Halfway out in the street, ignoring the honking cars swerving by, she wasn't a superwoman after all—just my mom, waving her arms and mouthing words that needed no sound for my heart to hear them.

For just an instant, all the anger and hurt that had filled me for weeks seemed to disappear. But it was just a fleeting moment, and that darn bus just kept right on going. At the end of the block, it rounded the corner and Mom was gone.

As the buildings flashed by on either side of the bus, I glanced down at my wristwatch. It was 6:57 A.M.

Right on time.

I had just turned thirteen a few weeks earlier. I guess that was right on time, too, for whatever awaited me. Not that I had any choice in the matter. You see, I'd been condemned to a terrible fate: I was on my way north to Seattle, exiled to spend an entire summer with a grandmother I didn't even know.

It didn't matter that I expected my dad back home any day, no matter what everyone was saying—that he'd never, ever come back.

It didn't matter that I was old enough to take care of myself while Mom was taking college classes and studying.

It didn't matter that I wouldn't be in the way.

It didn't matter that I didn't want to go.

Nothing I wanted seemed to matter to anybody, and especially not to my mom.

Maybe it had never mattered. But that was something I wasn't ready to consider. At least, not yet.

But Mom had it all figured out, wrapped up and decided like a Christmas present, no ifs, ands, or returns allowed.

So there I was, heading north, courtesy of that speedy old Greyhound.

It was June 11, 1970, and all I knew for certain on that foggy June morning, as that bus lumbered along, was that on my first time away from home by myself, I felt unloved, unwanted, and forgotten.

Oh, yeah, and I was spitting mad, too.

Giving up, I slumped back in my seat, bit my lip, fixed my eyes on the back of the bus driver's head, and tried to think about my next move.

But I couldn't get past the anger, ache, and despair burning in my heart. I just couldn't ignore the crazy jumble of thoughts that raced around inside my head.

*What had I done to deserve this*?

I wasn't a bad kid, not really.

Opinionated? Sure.

Smart-mouthed? Absolutely.

Sassy? Guilty as charged. But what thirteen-year-old girl isn't?

Of course, Mom and I argued. Did we ever! But what teenage daughter doesn't fight with her mom now and then? It's the ones who don't—the ones who coo that their mother is their best friend—that I've learned to be careful around.

No, the arguments between us had never been anything too serious—just the typical disagreements between moms and daughters about clothes, homework, school, and friends—at least not until that spring. That's when it had all changed. Suddenly, I couldn't do anything right. I think it had less to do with me and more to do with the news that Dad wasn't coming home anytime soon. Whatever the reason, I have never been one to back down from a fight, and neither has my mom.

She responded by doing something I didn't think I could ever forgive: sending me away from everyone and everything I loved. It made me wonder if Mom had ever really loved me in the first place.

And who could blame me?

As I sat there, trying to come to grips with what was happening to me, I began to cry, burying my head in my arms and trying not to make too much noise.

I guess I wasn't anywhere near as brave and tough and grown-up as I liked to think.

# Chapter Two

I was still sniffling a while later, when I heard some-one say, "Here, kid, take this."

I wiped my eyes with the back of my hand and glanced around. I assumed that somebody had had enough of my carrying on and decided to offer me a hanky so I could blow my nose, clean off my face, and shut up.

I glared at the man across the aisle. He was slumped in his seat, arms folded across his chest. He had an A's baseball cap pulled low over his eyes. *Not him*, I thought.

On his right, next to the window, was a soldier, look-ing neat and clean in his olive green dress uniform. He was staring straight ahead, his hair so short that it looked like sandpaper. I wondered if he knew my dad.

If he had been black instead of white, I would have said, "Say, mister, do you happen to know Master Sergeant James Thompson?" But you never could tell with white folks—I mean, how they might reply to a black kid. Some people were all friendly and nice, and others, who looked like they might be friendly and nice, would treat you like a dog—and talk to you even worse.

It wasn't like the bad old days of slavery, or even the days before Rosa Parks decided she wasn't going to give up her seat near the front of the bus. But it had been only two years since Dr. King was shot and killed by that white man. I was old enough to know that changing a law didn't necessarily change the way people thought or felt—or how they treated you.

So I kept quiet. I sneaked a peek through the gap between my seats at the people behind me. A plump woman, her hair piled up like an ice cream sundae, had the mirror out of her purse and was admiring the paint job on her face. The equally plump man next to her was just staring out the window, looking sad. I wondered if someone was making him go to Seattle, too. Or maybe he just needed a cup of coffee and another sweet roll.

"Can't hold it all day." That voice again.

Now that I'd stopped blubbering like a baby, I could tell what direction it was coming from. I whirled around, but instead of a hanky for my nose, the bus driver was wagging a purple Tootsie Pop over his right shoulder.

"No, thanks," I snapped, still a little angry about his earlier wisecrack comparing picking a seat to shoe shopping. And now he was treating me like some little kid.

"Sheesh," I added, under my breath.

"Suit yourself," the bus driver said, with an indifferent shrug.

I started having second thoughts as soon as he began to pull his hand back. After a few minutes, I couldn't stand it any longer. "How'd you know purple was my favorite?" I blurted.

"Lucky guess, I suppose," the bus driver replied. I noticed his face in the big mirror above the windshield. A smile was peeking out from beneath his moustache.

I glanced down at my purple sneakers with purple shoelaces, my faded purple bell-bottom jeans, and my purple tie-dyed T-shirt with the big green peace sign on the front. I reached up and fingered the matching purple tie-dyed bow in my bushy black hair.

"Go ahead," he said. His left hand remained locked on the big black steering wheel, while the other waved the sucker tantalizingly close to my nose. I could almost smell the grape-flavored candy.

When his voice dropped to a whisper, I had to lean forward in my seat to hear: "Just make sure you keep this between you and me."

I glanced again at the man across the aisle. He hadn't stirred. His mouth was hanging open, his jaw slack. The soldier was just staring out the window.

"Sure, mister," I whispered, a willing accomplice.

"You see, only my co-pilots, the ones in the seats right behind me, get one of these," he explained.

"Groovy," I said. And then I remembered my manners. "Thank you," I added, as I snatched the sucker from his hand.

"You're welcome," said the bus driver. When he popped a red one into his own mouth, the bond was sealed.

"My name is Gus. What's yours?"

"Maya," I said.

"Well, Miss Maya, I'm operating under direct orders from your mother. Gotta keep an eye on you. So you got any problems, you let me know. Okay?"

"Ah hum," was all I could murmur, my mouth already working on that purple Tootsie Pop. I wasn't all that surprised by his admission. In fact, it just confirmed my earlier suspicions.

I suppose it took me till I was about halfway to the soft chocolate center to start thinking that the bus ride part of this trip might not be as bad as I had expected.

I was still angry about going to Seattle, but I had always liked riding on school buses. Gus seemed nice enough, despite the fact that he was in cahoots with my mom. I just hoped he didn't ask me to look at a map—I wasn't any good at it.

I had tried to find South Vietnam on one of those National Geographic maps once. That's where my dad was stuck fighting in a war I still don't understand. I had found South Dakota, South Carolina, and South America on that stupid map before I finally gave up. Geography still isn't one of my strong points.

It wasn't until months later that I finally found out in school that South Vietnam was in Southeast Asia, all the way on the other side of the world, underneath Japan and South Korea. Seeing it there on the globe, I had finally realized for the first time just how far away my dad truly was. He could have been on another planet in another galaxy. Even the moon, something I gazed at nearly every night, seemed closer than South Vietnam.

My most prized possessions in the entire world were the letters Dad had sent me from so far away. I had them safely stashed in my backpack. I would never have gone away without them, because when I read my dad's letters, I could almost hear him whispering the words in my ear, his deep, warm voice making me feel safe and loved.

If Gus had to rely on my directions to Seattle, I'd have to warn him that we could end up just about anywhere! Of course, there was no sense worrying about that until he asked for help. I already had enough things on my mind.

No, I did not intend to take being banished to Seattle

lightly: when Mom had gone to the ladies' room at the bus station, I had cleaned out all the money in her purse.

Now I had some options. That was one of my dad's favorite words. "A person's gotta have *options* in life," I remember him saying, the night before he left for Vietnam. "That's what the Army has given me. Options for school if I want. Options for jobs when I get home." He must have seen the puzzled look on my face.

"It's another word for *choices*, Honey Bear," he said. "If you can only do one thing, that's no choice at all. But if you can pick from two or three or ten things, that's—"

"Options," I interrupted.

"You got it," he beamed.

So that's why I didn't see taking the money as stealing. I figured it served Mom right for the way she'd treated me. Nope, I was just following my dad's advice, making sure I had a few options—in the form of $38.53, hidden away in the secret pocket of my backpack.

If my grandma turned out to be a cranky old witch living in a stinky old house that smelled of cat, there was no way I was going to stay put there.

It was right about then, thinking about my dad in Vietnam and the terrible way my mom was acting, that I started feeling lonely and mad all over again.

Trying not to cry, I bit down on my lower lip hard

enough to draw blood. There'd be no more blubbering; I had done enough of that already, and it was time to act my age. But pretending to cry again might have some advantages, especially if I cranked it up and just cut loose like one of those soap opera actresses, howling and yowling.

Maybe I could squeeze another sucker out of old Gus. And who knows what the other passengers might give me to shut me up? Like my best friend Elizabeth always said, "Only the squeaky wheel gets the grease."

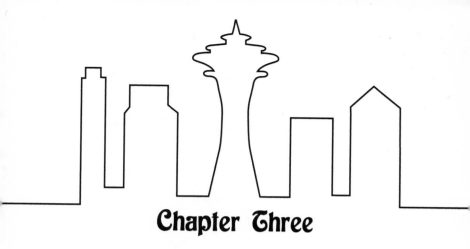

# Chapter Three

"You know what they call Seattle?"

I kept silent, figuring Gus would glance in his mirror and realize I was right in the middle of tallying up my hard-earned booty. I wasn't trying to be rude, but if I paused to reply, I would lose count and have to start all over again.

I was feeling kind of proud of myself. In a performance worthy of an Academy Award, I'd managed to howl, sob, and whimper for a solid half hour—long enough to motivate most of my fellow travelers to send candy, comics, and other assorted goodies my way—in hopes of shutting me up. By my tally, I now had enough stuff to last me all the way to Seattle, and then some.

The bus was making a beeline through the state of Oregon by this point, past forests, farmlands, and fields, with the occasional small town flashing by. Everything—even the towns—had a fresh, scrubbed look.

"Nice haul," Gus commented.

"Excuse me?" I asked.

"I said, nice haul. Little old for all that carrying on, so I wondered how you'd do. And switching back and forth between crying and whimpering—that was a nice touch."

"Thank you," I said automatically.

"I was also wondering how long you would be able to keep at it. Nowhere near the record, though," he teased.

"What do you mean?" I asked.

"Had a baby with an earache that cried solid for nine hours on this trip a while back. Poor critter. Darn near drove everyone on the bus crazy. After we arrived, I thought somebody was going to get killed in the stampede to get off."

I imagined a crazed bus driver piloting a bus filled with wild-eyed passengers. It would make a good horror movie. Forget monsters from Mars or a bus with a couple of thirsty vampire passengers. Just bring on a baby with a sore ear, stand back, and watch the commotion begin.

"Did you go crazy, too?" I asked.

Gus fished around in his shirt pocket and pulled out a couple of fluorescent orange earplugs connected by a matching string. He held them up and grinned into the mirror at me.

"I was wondering why you didn't get mad at me for bawling so long," I said.

Gus shrugged, as if it was something he'd dealt with a thousand times before. Who knows? Maybe he had.

"So, you know what they call Seattle?" he asked again.

I popped a peppermint candy into my mouth and thought. "Windy City?" I guessed, imagining a tornado sweeping down out of the sky and sucking Seattle up its throat. Now, that definitely would solve my problem.

Gus laughed and shook his head. "No, that's Chicago. Try again."

"Stinkyville?" I asked, mischievously.

"Aren't you the little whip," Gus quipped. "Nope, that'd be Tacoma. Pulp plant makes the air thick 'nough to taste. It's mighty close to Seattle, though. When it starts to stink, you'll know we're almost there. One more try."

I thought for a moment, trying to remember everything I knew about Seattle. It wasn't much. Mom had grown up there. She had left when she and my dad ran off and got married. He had just turned eighteen. She was seventeen. They never went back. Never.

Every once in a while, she talked about how much she missed the mountains and the lakes, the beaches and the rain. Her voice was always sad with memory, along with something else I could not put my finger on. But she didn't often mention her childhood home or talk about her mom—my grandmother.

I couldn't come up with an answer that was smart-alecky enough, so I shrugged and said, "I give up."

"Queen City," Gus said. "That's what they call it."

"Why?" I asked.

Now it was Gus's turn to shrug. "I dunno. But I like my nickname better."

"What's that?" I shot back.

"The Emerald City."

"Like in *The Wizard of Oz?*"

Gus nodded. "But I call it that 'cause it's so green. You know why that is, don't you?"

"Fertilizer," I blurted out, thinking about the powder my mom used to keep her houseplants green and healthy.

"Nope," Gus said, sounding serious all of a sudden. "It's because it rains all the time, that's why. And if you're not careful, you could end up with webbed feet just like a duck."

"Awww-gooo-onnn," snorted the man across the aisle. He reached up to tug on the bill of his baseball cap, but then glanced across the aisle when his fingers found nothing but air. I could tell he was having second thoughts about his shut-up bribe by the way he eyed his A's baseball cap, now on my head.

He pulled his eyes away from my new cap with obvious effort. "He ain't right," he said. "It only rains *most* of the time."

They both started laughing at the joke. As soon as I realized it wasn't about me, I joined in. It felt good to laugh again.

The next few hours passed quickly. Gus and I spent most of the time talking about baseball, and books, and our families. By the time we reached Corvallis, Oregon, I'd started explaining why I was on the bus.

"It's her fault," I said.

I saw Gus's eyes flick up to the rearview mirror, then back to the road. I took it as a cue that he was listening and that it was okay to continue.

"You see, she's trying to finish her college degree," I began.

"And that's not a good thing?" he said.

"No, no, it's good. It's just that she said she didn't want me home alone, causing who knows what kind of mischief, while she was taking classes or studying. In other words, I was going to be in the way."

"Well, would you?" Gus asked.

"Would I what?" I asked.

"Cause trouble?" he replied. "You know, dress like a hippie, smoke dope, and sit around all day listening to that god-awful howling they call music."

"Of course not," I said, noticing his eyes crinkle in the corners as he grinned.

"I'm old enough to take care of myself," I said hotly. "But her mind was made up. Simple as that. All her friends were too busy to keep an eye on me. As if I need a babysitter." I spit out that last word with venom.

"So then what happened?" Gus asked.

"That left the only person who could take me for the summer," I snarled.

"Who's that?" he asked.

"My grandmother," I groaned.

"And what's wrong with that?" Gus said.

"Everything!" I exploded. "I don't know her. I can't ever remember visiting her. She's . . . she's a total stranger."

"So now you get a chance to know her," Gus said, with a shrug, as if it was no big deal.

"But don't you think it's kind of weird that we've never, ever visited her?" I asked him.

"Some people don't like to travel," Gus said. "Not that I understand it."

"What about her?" I almost shouted. "She's never visited us, either."

"Did you ask your mother about it?" he questioned softly.

"I tried once," I said. "She said I wouldn't understand. She said I was too young . . . and then she changed the subject."

"So, let me get this straight," Gus said, lifting one hand from the wheel and jabbing the air. "You've never visited your grandma. And she's never visited you. You've never talked to her on the telephone. And your mother never, ever talks about her?"

"That's about right," I said, with a nod. For an adult, he was a pretty good listener.

"Sounds like you're stuck with a normal family to me," he said, with a laugh.

I stuck out my tongue at him. "Every once in a long while, Mom mentions her name. But then she gets the saddest look on her face. If you didn't know better, you'd think she was talking about somebody who was dead. What kind of family acts like that, huh?"

I figured that right about now was when I'd get the typical grown-up lecture. Gus would decide he needed to say that she was right and I was wrong. That I was being unreasonable. That it wasn't easy being a parent nowadays. That I should cut her some slack. But after a few moments of quiet, he just nodded and said he imagined it must be hard on both of us.

Of course, I still hadn't revealed my real, deep-down fear.

You see, I'd always wondered if the problem between Mom and my grandmother had something to do with me. Maybe my grandmother just didn't like me, and that was the reason we never saw her.

My best friend Elizabeth had said that I probably had peed on my grandma when she was changing my diaper. That's what she guessed had set off Grandma and Mom.

But I told Elizabeth she was crazy. Everybody knew that babies sometimes had accidents. They were babies, for goodness' sake, and it was dumb to blame them for something they couldn't help doing.

By the end of my retort, Elizabeth was doubled over laughing. That was one reason she was my best friend. She could always make a joke out of the most serious things.

But I wondered afterwards if there was a nub of truth to what Elizabeth had joked about. Maybe it did have something to do with me. Maybe something about me had made Grandma hate us.

On the other hand, she didn't hate us so much that she forgot to send birthday cards and Christmas presents. I supposed that was something. But cards and presents don't mean very much when you don't sense any warmth and affection coming with them.

Eventually, I'd decided that she was a dried-up piece of cow you-know-what, one who didn't like me and Mom.

So I wasn't going to care about her one way or another, either, thank you very much.

As the morning turned into afternoon, I discovered that Gus and I shared many interests. Who would have guessed it? An old, bald-headed white bus driver and a thirteen-year-old black girl liked the same things.

Well, mostly the same things. I loved chocolate marble ice cream. Gus liked strawberry. But I didn't hold strawberry against him, and he didn't hold chocolate marble against me.

We both loved baseball, reading, and music. Unfortunately, he was a San Francisco Giants fan, while my favorite team was the Oakland A's. I think he was surprised to find a girl who loved baseball.

"Who's your pick for the Series this year?" he asked.

"The Mets won't repeat," I said.

"Got that right," he agreed, with a laugh. "That was a miracle. Maybe they'll do it again in a hundred years."

"Well, I'd love to say the A's, but my dad thinks it's going to be Baltimore, so I'll go with them."

"Baltimore?" Gus snorted derisively. "You'd better have a little chat with your daddy—set him straight, if you know what I mean." Gus glanced up in the mirror and winked.

We told each other about our favorite books. He liked

reading history books about people and places from long ago.

I wrinkled my nose at that. I said I liked to read stories about animals and Indians.

"Nancy Drew?" he asked.

I shrugged. "They're okay. She always seems a little prissy," I said.

I told him that I was part Indian—Cherokee, to be exact.

He asked me which part. Ear? Nose?

"Big toe," I said.

As for music, I liked playing the piano well enough—mostly classical music, because that's what my teacher, Mrs. Friermuth, made me play. But my favorite at that moment was an electric guitar player named Jimi Hendrix.

"That's Jimi with one 'm,' and it ends in an 'i,'" I said.

"Sounds like a girl's name," Gus sniffed. "Never heard of him. Electric guitar, you say?"

I nodded.

"Rock music?"

I nodded again.

"That's too bad," Gus said. "I do like to hear a good electric guitar." When Gus said the word *guitar*, he pronounced it "gee-tar."

I mentioned that my mom happened to like a singer

who I knew by only one name: Aretha. I thought she was okay, too. But mostly I liked the words to her songs.

"Mel Tormé!" Gus said. "Now that's a singer. Don't forget my all-time favorite, Ella Fitzgerald. And what about Duke Ellington—and Dave Brubeck?"

Now it was my turn. "Never heard of them!" I said. "What kind of music do they play?"

Gus gave me a look of disbelief. "Ever heard of jazz?"

I shrugged. "Sure. Mom plays it sometimes. I asked Mrs. Friermuth about it once, but she made a noise in the back of her throat that sounded like she was trying to cough up a hairball. I didn't ask again."

Gus shook his head and muttered. "Of all the crazy . . ."

"How 'bout your daddy?" Gus asked.

"He's in the Army," I said, glancing at the soldier across the aisle. He was leaning against the window, his face turned away from me. He looked like he was asleep. "And right now he's in Vietnam," I insisted, "and doing just fine, too. I worry about him a lot, but he promised me he'd be okay and come home soon, so I don't believe—"

I caught myself before I repeated what everyone else had been saying, including my mom. It was not true. None of it. I knew it deep down in my heart. And I wasn't going to help make it real by saying it—or even *thinking* it.

I took a shaky breath and forced a smile. "Actually," I continued, "I expect him home any time now. He writes that he's doing fine and can't wait to get home."

Gus was watching me, his brow furrowed, his eyes dark and hot. "I see," he said in such a way that I wondered if maybe my mom had told him something.

"I was in the Army," he said, after a while. "But they sent me to a place called South Korea."

"Was it hot there, like in South Vietnam?"

"Nope. It was cold. Very, very cold." I saw his shoulders shake with a remembered shiver. "Winter there was like spending time in a meat locker without a coat or shoes. Sometimes we were so cold, we didn't dare fall asleep at night."

"Why not?"

I saw his lips moving in the mirror above the windshield.

"What was that?"

"I was afraid I wouldn't ever wake up again!" he shouted, his face suddenly red with emotion. "We all were, 'cept the ones who didn't care anymore." I noticed the soldier across the aisle watching us now, fumbling with a pack of cigarettes. He stared blankly at me for half a second, and then his eyes drifted back outside.

It took a moment before I realized what Gus had just said. When it sank in, I couldn't hold back a shiver of my own.

I wondered if freezing to death hurt very much. Maybe it was as gentle as falling asleep. You would be cold at first, but then you'd quit shivering, and before long, you would just drift off. I never got a chance to ask. He kept right on talking—to himself as much as to me. I knew the feeling.

"When I finally came home," he said, "it took me six solid months to thaw out and feel warm again. I couldn't eat strawberry ice cream for years. Reminded me too much of Korea and all that cold." Gus shuddered again, remembering.

"But you didn't fall asleep," I said, my voice tight. "You came back."

Gus nodded. "And don't you worry about your father," he continued, with a shake of his head. "I 'spect any father of yours is sure to take good care of himself."

After that, Gus was quiet for a while. I saw him glance at me every now and then, chewing on his lip, as if he wanted to say some more. But he didn't.

I spent some time drawing pictures on a sketch pad. I even started a letter to Elizabeth and another one to Dad. But it's hard to draw or write in a moving bus—too much shaking and jiggling. I gave up and read for a while, then finally quit and just looked out the window.

Occasionally, a town would flash by, frozen for just a moment, as if someone was holding up a gigantic postcard outside my window. I'd see cars and people, buildings with smoke curling out of the chimneys, dogs hustling down alleyways, and then it would all be gone, replaced by the rhythmic pulse of passing fields and trees and farms.

When my eyelids grew heavy, I curled up on my seat like a cat and slept, surprised at how safe I felt with Gus the bus driver watching over me.

And that's how it went as the bus rolled steadily north, gulping the miles as it moved.

I didn't think about where I was going. I didn't even worry about meeting the grandmother I didn't know or what would happen when I did.

If truth be told, I wouldn't have minded if that Greyhound bus had just kept going on forever.

# Chapter Four

"Say hello to Seattle," she said.

I hid a giggle with the back of my hand, wondering why Elizabeth's voice had suddenly dropped two octaves. Elizabeth must have wondered, too. Her eyes widened in surprise, and she started to say something I knew was important; but then, just like that, she was gone, the dream pushed aside by a gasp from the bus's air brakes.

I didn't want to wake up. I wasn't ready to face what was coming. But like a frog spiraling toward the surface of a pond, I had no time to stop and worry about what might be waiting in the world above the surface. I suppose I was hoping that if I kept my eyes closed tight, I could stay safely below the surface, dreaming all the while that I was still back home with Elizabeth and not on a bus arriving in Seattle.

But Elizabeth always said—it was one of her famous rules of the universe—that the harder you try to stay asleep, the more awake you become. She was right. A rule is a rule.

I reluctantly opened my eyes and sat up.

First, I pushed my hair out of the way and turned toward the back of the bus. Everyone was already out of their seats, crowding into the aisle. They were chattering happily, a few yawning and stretching, most reaching for bags and suitcases on the racks overheard.

Next, I heard the door whoosh open. It sounded like a can of vacuum-sealed peanuts opening.

I wrinkled my nose at the mixture of city smells that suddenly poured into the bus. The air smelled a bit like home, but it was different enough to be distinct—saltier and spicier, with a hint of evergreen and ripe garbage.

"Seattle," Gus barked into his microphone again, as if anyone needed a reminder where we were. I couldn't understand why bus drivers announced the name of the city when they arrived. Everyone with half a brain already knew we were in Seattle, not San Antonio or Las Vegas. If they didn't, then they deserved to be in the wrong city.

But like it or not, his words warned me that it was time to go. I gathered the things I'd scattered around the seat and floor, stuffing them into my backpack as fast as I could. Then I dumped everything back out onto the seat, only to put it all back in again, this time neatly and carefully.

Of course, I was dawdling, trying my best to avoid the inevitable. I didn't want to get off the bus, and now that it was time, I was getting that all-alone feeling again.

And there was something else, too, that I don't mind admitting now. It was fear, plain and simple: I was deathly afraid of my unknown grandmother.

Afraid of what had happened between her and Mom.

Afraid she'd be mean.

Afraid she'd think I was stupid.

Afraid she'd take one look at me and decide, right then and there, that . . .

"You all right, Maya?" Gus asked, breaking the spell.

I blinked a couple of times and then swallowed hard.

Gus gave me a tired smile. "It's going to be all right," he insisted, as the last person brushed past my seat and disappeared down the steps.

"I'll be sure and look for you in a couple of months on the return trip. Maybe I'll be lucky enough to drive your bus again," he added, with a wink.

"Thanks," I said, finding my voice and straining to return his smile, almost believing him.

"My pleasure," Gus laughed, taking off his cap and bowing like a knight in days of old.

Then it was my turn. With one last wave to Gus, I trudged down the steps and off the bus, suddenly feeling very small and frightened. I wondered if this was how a chick feels, breaking through an eggshell and seeing the world for the first time.

The big clock above the glass doors of the bus terminal said it was almost midnight. But the place was bustling with people and lit up like daytime by the bright lights over the huge parking lot, where buses were either letting out their passengers or waiting for the next group to board.

Across the way, next to the curb, a line of dirty yellow taxis idled, waiting for newly arriving customers. Some of the drivers, leaning out of their windows, were smoking cigarettes and staring at us like a line of hungry seagulls.

Beyond the taxis, I could see gray and shadowed streets, punctuated here and there by entrances to dark alleys.

I hated dark alleys. They were such narrow, dirty, creepy places, usually filled with rats and big, ugly spiders. I shivered and hugged my backpack close to my chest.

Where was she? What if she had forgotten about me and was snoozing away in her bed? Or maybe she was off somewhere with her friends, playing bingo and sipping tea. Or maybe she was here after all, somewhere in the crowd that pressed against the glass doors of the terminal. But what if she didn't recognize me? How would I recognize her?

Hours seemed to pass while I stood there, waiting, worrying, and fretting. It's funny how time can shrink or stretch, depending on what you're doing or thinking. I suspect that only an instant actually passed before I heard the words "There you are!"

The voice was sharp as a knife, and it instantly reminded me of Mom's, only older and raspier.

I turned my head and saw her, standing off by herself to my right. She was partly hidden by a cart loaded with boxes and suitcases.

At first glance, I could see that Grandma was no dried-up hunk of cow poop after all, but instead a tall, dark-skinned woman wearing a navy blue dress that fit her like a uniform. She was an older, thicker version of my mom. She wore a small, round hat perched on top of her thick, graying hair, which was coiled up like a snake. The way she clutched her purse made her look like she was on her way to church.

"Yes, ma'am?" I squeaked, feeling a sense of relief so strong it made my knees weak.

"Welcome to Seattle," she said, stepping closer, all the while looking me right in the eyes.

For just a heartbeat, I was happy to see her. But then she held out her hand for me to shake and I remembered that we were a couple of strangers. "You were just a little baby the last time I saw you," she remarked, her words like sand blowing against my soul.

I didn't know what to say. A handshake? Maybe she really did hate me. I guess I didn't know enough to hate her back, at least not yet. I grabbed her hand awkwardly, pumping it up and down as all the feelings and worries came flooding back.

I tried to return her gaze, to show her that I was not afraid. But her look seemed to cut right through me. I wondered if she had the gift, if she could tell what I was thinking without my saying a word.

I screamed out the words in my mind: *I HATE YOU! I HATE YOU. . . . I HATE YOU!*

Her expression didn't change. "I see you like purple," she announced, with the precision of an old-fashioned schoolteacher.

*I guess you can't read my mind*, I thought.

"Cat got your tongue?"

"Yes'm," I croaked. "I mean, yeah, purple is cool."

"Your mother's favorite color was red," she remarked, more to herself than to me.

"Still is," I replied.

Grandma pursed her lips and nodded. "That is no surprise. She is not one to change her mind once it's made up."

Oh, yes! I knew all about that! So, we had something in common after all—not that it was going to matter.

"How many suitcases?" my grandma asked.

"Just one," I whispered.

She nodded as if I'd given the right answer to a test. "Very well, then, let's go get it. It is well past my bedtime. Yours, too, I should hope."

As I followed her into the terminal, Dad's favorite word tumbled through my mind: *options*. I could almost feel Mom's money waiting in the backpack. It certainly gave me an option or two. I could walk right into her house and follow her into whatever tiny closet or tool shed she'd planned as my bedroom. Of course, I would never stay put. I would wait for her to close the door, and then I'd keep right on going, out the window, across the lawn, and down the street. I could be on the next bus to Chicago before she ever knew otherwise.

On the other hand, I was old enough to know that running away brought its own complications. Where would I go? My best friend Elizabeth was spending the summer in Chicago. She had said I could stay with her. But Mom had vetoed that idea every time I asked her. "Too far away" was her excuse.

I had pointed out the obvious—that South Vietnam was too far away, but Chicago wasn't much farther away than Seattle, especially when you're starting from San Francisco. What was another day or two on a damn bus?

Her response to my irrefutable, unassailable logic was to send me to my room for "using foul language and talking back." What-ever!

I suspected she had other reasons for not wanting me to spend time with Elizabeth. Elizabeth's mother was black, but her father was white. Sometimes, that caused problems when they were together. And not just with whites. Some black folks didn't like it, either. Maybe Mom wasn't as open and accepting as she liked to pretend. When I thought about running away, I realized that Chicago would have to be my last option.

But there might be another, more direct way to get back home. I must confess that thinking about it was enough to make me smile, really smile, for what felt like the first time in a long while. I wasn't going to run off, not unless I was forced to. But I was finished with doing what people expected. If I was going to stay put, I was going to do what I wanted to do. If that made Grandma's life miserable or a living hell, then so be it. If I handled it right, maybe she would give up and send me back home, without my even asking. Then Mom would be forced to take me back. I could even imagine that Grandma might slip a few dollars in my pocket on my way out the door.

I started to whistle through my teeth. Summer no longer seemed so bleak. If I played my cards right, I might even be home by the All-Star Game.

Grandma glanced over her shoulder and frowned, wondering, I'm sure, why I was feeling so chipper.

I replied with a smile. The poor old woman had no idea what she was in for—yet.

# Chapter Five

The stranger-who-was-my-grandmother stalked back and forth, looking over those taxis like she couldn't decide which old-lady bra to pick out.

She finally settled on the yellow Ford right in the middle, waving her hand in the air to shoo away the squawks from the first cabbie in line.

When the other cabbie heard her order the "lucky" choice to put out his cigarette and crank open all the windows before she would agree to climb inside, his objections turned to derisive laughter. "Good riddance, lady!" he yelled in our direction.

I could tell right off that our cabbie didn't like being ordered around by an old woman and then teased by his buddies. He smiled back at my grandma in a way that was no smile at all and then opened all the windows. "Where to, lady?"

"Capitol Hill," Grandma said, snipping out those

words as if she was cutting out a dress pattern. "Corner of 17th and Beech."

"Right-o," he growled, stomping on the accelerator.

"And so, young lady, how was the bus ride?" Grandma asked. *Snip. Snip. Snip.*

"Long," I snipped back.

"How is your mother's health?"

"Fine . . . I guess."

I could sense that she'd turned her head, staring at me in the darkness.

"I see," she said, finally.

I'm sure she had no idea what was going on, and despite the way she'd eyed me when we first met, her actually "seeing" was something else altogether. But no matter what, after the long day on the bus, I wasn't in the mood for being grilled like some young girl caught stealing nail polish from the drugstore.

I took a deep breath, ready to cut loose with some serious San Francisco attitude in reply to her next question.

"Driving a taxi, that's just my fill-in job," the taxi driver blustered, before she had a chance to ask me any more questions.

"Ah-hmmm," Grandma replied, staring hard at the permit with the cabbie's name and picture on it that was pasted on the window.

"See, I'm a boxer," he said proudly.

"And what do you box?" Grandma asked.

The boxing cab driver glanced in the rearview mirror, just to make sure Grandma wasn't making fun of him. He must have been satisfied by what he saw. "Anything I can find," he said, with a snort of laughter, swiping at his nose with his thumb, "but mostly men."

"Mostly?" Grandma replied, with ice in her voice. "You mean the others you box are women and children?"

There was dead silence for a moment. "No," the cabbie replied sullenly.

"Indeed."

"I . . . I was just kidding," he stammered. "That's not what I meant. You see, there's punching bags and . . . "

"No one's laughing back here," I interrupted, deciding that Grandma shouldn't have all the fun.

I felt Grandma's hand light for just a moment on my arm.

The cabbie took a deep breath, then decided to forge ahead. "I'm a professional," he said. "You probably heard of me. Fightin' Frank McKenzie."

"Can't say I have," Grandma replied. "But I don't follow fisticuffs."

"Fistawhat?"

"Boxing."

"Ah. That's a new one." He barked out short laugh. "How 'bout you?" he challenged.

"I'm new here," I volunteered.

That seemed to satisfy him. "Well, ladies," he said, "y'all bein' chauffeured by the sixth-ranked heavyweight fighter in the entire Pacific Northwest hisself. That means I'm one of the best around these parts, so you is safe with me. And I expect to be movin' up. Gimme another year or two and one big fight, and I'll be making the big money. Do that for a few years, then no more cabs. No. I'll buy me a big-ass boat and spend my time fishing and crabbing in the Sound, just like those rich white folks."

"That'll be the day," I said sarcastically.

"Wha' was that?" he snapped.

"And I'm going to be the first black Miss America," I said.

He tilted his head and glanced over his shoulder, ready to give me the "What for?"

Grandma grabbed my arm again, squeezing hard enough this time that I had to stifle a squawk. "Are you a God-fearing man, Mr. McKenzie?" she interrupted.

The cabbie's eyes flicked up to the rearview mirror and then back to the road. "I s'pose so," he said cautiously.

"And where do you attend church on Sunday?" When Grandma asked that question, she made her voice sound real nice and pleasant-like.

"Well, ma'am," he stammered. "You know, I work

most weekends, and so I haven't settled on a congregation."

"What about Wednesday night church meeting?"

"Work evenings, too. Ain't easy to make a buck in this town. That's why I'm boxing. Just a few more fights, and I'm going to have a name for myself, and then—"

Grandma didn't let him get any further. She hit him with a sharp jab: "I see!"

"But I'm looking for a congregation," he said, struggling up to the very last.

Grandma moved in for the kill. "You must not be looking hard enough," she slugged, her nose lifting in the air with disdain. "I would like to invite you to worship with us at the Mt. Zion Holy Baptist Tabernacle and Church of God. I will keep an eye out for you this coming Sunday."

"I'll think about it," the cabbie muttered.

Church? I almost moaned with despair. One more thing to add to my list of things to be mad about. *Thanks for the warning, Mom*, I thought bitterly.

We bounced through a few intersections, the traffic lights blinking yellow as cat eyes in the dark. The driver reached forward to turn on the radio, but then he hesitated, careful to ask permission from Grandma first.

She didn't mind, as long as he kept it low or tuned it to a station that played decent, Christian music.

"Yes, ma'am," he replied, not asking what that might

be. In any case, I figured he set the dial on a station that played indecent music, because he kept it so quiet I couldn't even hear it in the back seat.

As we steadily made our way uphill, it reminded me of San Francisco. My city was famous for all its ups and downs. In fact, it is a place with so many ups and downs it's hard to find a flat place to kick a ball.

When I was a kid, Elizabeth and I were playing with a ball on the steep street in front of the apartment building where we lived. We'd take turns kicking the ball up the hill, wait for it to roll back, and then kick it again.

And then I missed, kicking too soon. That ball slipped right underneath my foot. I almost landed on it as my leg kept right on going. I flipped up in the air, then hit the pavement, landing flat on my back.

Elizabeth let out a squeal and lunged at the ball, but she was too late. I flopped over on my stomach and watched that ball careen downhill like a gigantic, out-of-control pinball, bumping into cars, curbs, and fire hydrants as it rolled.

As we sat there in the dark, I wondered what ever happened to that ball. From the way it was heading when it finally disappeared from sight, I figured it rolled all the way to San Francisco Bay.

I thought about asking Grandma for her opinion on

the matter, but one glance in her direction changed my mind. She was staring straight ahead, sitting stiffly, like she was too good to let the seat dirty the back of her coat.

She was quiet the rest of the ride. I suppose she was tired, too. Or maybe she had caught a glimpse of what was coming, wondering what she was going to do with a handful named Maya.

Before long, the big buildings were replaced by darkened houses passing by on either side. Their shadows were interrupted now and then by a strobe of porch lights, yellow against the black night, then gone as the taxi bounced along, always up and up.

At the top of the hill, the driver wheeled sharply to the right and pulled to a halt against the curb. He was out of the car in a flash and already had the suitcase waiting on the sidewalk by the time I slammed my door closed.

"Three fifty," the taxi driver said, shifting uncomfortably from foot to foot.

My grandmother fished through her purse and handed him a five-dollar bill.

"Thank you," he said, turning to leave.

"One minute," she said.

That stopped him dead in his tracks. No smile this time as he turned around.

"I think you owe me some change?"

"Uh, yeah, right," the driver snarled, fumbling in his pocket and then slapping a dollar bill and two quarters in her open palm. He looked up at me as he slid behind the wheel. "Good luck, kid. You're gonna need it."

"You got that right," I muttered.

"What did you say, Maya?" Grandma asked.

"Nothin'," I said, my shrug sugared with a fake smile.

Somebody in this house was going to need some luck. But it wasn't going to be me.

I followed my grandmother up the front steps. She unlocked the door. I followed her inside, hesitating at the doorway like a wild horse suspecting a trap. I sniffed the air, ready to plug my nose. But instead of stinking like an old lady's house, it had the stale odor of someplace long abandoned. I imagined it was filled with dust bunnies in the corners, with fat, sleepy mice and long-forgotten memories that sighed with longing whenever it was windy outside. I wondered when she had last opened the windows to let the breezes ruffle the curtains and blow away the past. It must have been years.

"You are probably wondering about the lemon?"

I sniffed again and sneezed. I couldn't smell anything like the pungent, mouthwatering odor of fresh lemon, but I nodded anyway.

"Wood polish," she said. "There's also a lemon meringue pie in the kitchen."

Now it was my turn to stare hard at her, spooked by how she happened to know that I loved lemon meringue pie. Of course, it was no gift or feat of magic. Mom had probably filled her in, simple as that.

Grandma carried my suitcase upstairs, flicking on the lights as she went. At the top of the stairs, we turned right and walked down the hallway. "You sleep in here," she said, pushing open a door and gesturing for me to follow. "This was—"

"Mom's room," I said softly, finishing her sentence. I knew it right off. The bright red quilt on the bed, the bookcase against the far wall, filled with the kind of books she liked, out-of-date pictures and posters hanging on the walls.

Grandma gave a short nod. "It is mostly the same as when your mother lived here. I had no reason to change it," she added, "though we may want to see about finding something else to cover the bed with, something maybe—"

"More purplish?" I suggested, hiding a yawn with the back of my hand.

She looked me up and down as if seeing me for the first time. "Perhaps," she said softly.

# Chapter Six

I woke the next morning to the sounds of pots and pans banging and clanging faintly from somewhere below. Sun was streaming through the window of my mom's room. Birds were chuckling and clucking like excited clowns in the branches of a big tree outside the window.

I yawned and stretched, wondering what Grandma would think if I found a good book and just stayed put, spending the morning lazing and reading in Mom's old bed. After last night's handshake, I wondered if she would even care.

There was another possibility. Just the thought of it almost made me giggle. Since she was probably older than many antiques, she might have forgotten I was even here, that late-night memory of me and the bus lost like a dream in the morning. I imagined how it would be: I'd show up downstairs and she'd shriek with terror and surprise, chasing me out of the house with a broom before I had a chance to remind her who I was.

The ruckus below continued, growing loud enough to get my attention again. My grumbling stomach made the final decision. I rolled out of bed, still yawning, and followed the noise downstairs.

At first, I stood in the kitchen doorway, rubbing my eyes, watching. Grandma had pots and pans strewn across the black- and-white checkered linoleum floor. She was down on her hands and knees, peering into the bottom cabinet.

"Where are you, you—" she warbled hoarsely, until she noticed me. "Oh, it's you." Her voice and mood changed so suddenly that it made me wonder if she had a switch hidden somewhere.

"Happy to see you, too," I muttered.

"Pardon?" she said, climbing stiffly to her feet, wiping her hands on the front of her bright yellow apron.

"Yeah, it's just little ol' me," I said glumly. "Nobody else."

She must have realized how she had sounded in the echo of my response. "I am not used to having visitors," she said, with a wave of her hand. I suppose it was as close to an apology as I was going to get. "How did you sleep?"

"All right, I guess," I said, with feigned indifference, waiting as long as I could, hoping she would provide an explanation and save me from having to ask her myself.

52

When she showed no inclination of filling me in, I finally burst out, "Mind telling me what on earth is going on?"

"Mice," she said, "or as your mom called them when she was just a little one, 'meeces.' " I saw a smile creep across her face at the memory and then fade before it even had a chance to get going. "Ever since Franklin Roosevelt passed away, they have become a real nuisance," she said, as if she was talking to herself. "I am now finding them in just about everything. Messy, filthy little rodents."

"Franklin Roosevelt?"

"Yes, yes," she said, with an impatient wave of her hand. "I named him in honor of President Franklin D. Roosevelt. My daddy—your great-grandfather—admired him greatly."

I nodded. "So somebody you named after a dead president of the United States died recently." I repeated it slowly to myself, trying to get it straight, wondering if I was missing something.

"He was my cat," she added, as if it was the punch line to a joke. But she didn't crack a smile, and so neither did I.

Sure. A cat. I suppose I should have guessed it. On the other hand, I was tired and hungry, and it did seem kind of kooky that she had named a cat after a dead president of the United States.

She didn't look that old, but maybe she was already beginning to go senile. I wondered if my mom had any idea what she was really like. Probably not. She didn't have a clue about me, so how would she know anything about someone she hadn't seen in so many years?

"Get another one?" I suggested.

"Excuse me?"

"Get . . . another . . . cat," I said slowly, like I was talking to a child or an idiot.

My grandma looked down at the pots and pans. "Of course, that would be the sensible thing," she said to herself with a nod. "Or call an exterminator. But I hate the thought of having all that poison lying around the place." She shuddered.

"So get another cat," I said again, wondering why the decision was so difficult and whether she was going to offer me any breakfast or if she was waiting for me to get down on my knees and beg. "I don't think Franklin Jefferson Washington or whatever you called him would be upset or anything. After all, he was just a cat."

"Franklin D. Roosevelt, you mean!" my grandma said sharply. "That was his name. And he wasn't just *any* cat."

"Whatever," I muttered.

Her eyes flashed a warning.

"Why don't you just name your new cat after another president?" I suggested.

"No, I could never replace Franklin D. Roosevelt," my grandma replied. "Ever," she added, glaring in my direction.

That was when I realized that my campaign of disruption and mischief had already begun. If I was lucky, I might be on the bus back home by the end of the week. I hoped Mom would think twice before trying to send me away again after this.

"Nope, a cat is exactly what you need." In an inspired bit of genius, I added, "It's what Franklin would have wanted."

Grandma didn't want another cat. She'd made that very clear. But in my new, mixed-up world of opposites, that meant it was the perfect time to push her into getting one. I would insist. She wouldn't dare disappoint her only granddaughter. Not on her first full day in town.

"You think so?" she said, cocking her head to one side like a bird.

I nodded. I should have stopped, but I prattled on, nearly ruining everything. "I think we should get one today, in fact. It would be so cool. And what about calling him . . . Richard Nixon?"

Grandma's response was immediate. Her face dissolved into wrinkles. "I have never liked that man," she said. "I did not like him when he was vice president to Mr. Dwight David Eisenhower, I did not like him the first time he ran for president and lost, and I do not like him now. There is something, well, sneaky about him."

*That's the least of his faults*, I thought, forced to agree with her on all of her points. Like many kids my age, I hated the current president, Richard M. Nixon, his right-hand gargoyle, Henry Kissinger, and all the rest of those warmongers. They'd promised to get us out of that war in Vietnam, but my dad was still over there fighting. And that TV news reporter guy, Walter somebody, who my friend Elizabeth said looked just like a walrus, was still reading his daily and yearly totals of dead and missing at the end of every newscast.

Of course, he had the wrong number for his yearly total. It was off by one. I'd written CBS letters about it, pointing out their mistake about my dad. They hadn't bothered to reply. I guess I wasn't important enough for them to issue a correction.

"Sneaky sounds exactly right for a cat," I said, giving it one more try.

My grandma crossed her arms and shook her head back and forth like a stubborn mule. But I did notice one thing. At least, now she was objecting to a name, not the idea of getting another cat.

"Well, then, how about calling him, oh, I don't know, Harry Truman?" I suggested the first name that popped into my head. I wasn't sure if it was the name of a former president of the United States or the man who sold used cars in San Jose and was always cackling away on the radio and TV.

Of course, by now, I was beginning to care less and less about a name for a cat. My stomach was getting impatient and letting me know it. Even a bowl of overcooked mush was beginning to sound tasty.

"Now, there was a fine man," my grandma agreed, holding her chin with her fingers as she considered the idea. "Mr. Harry S. Truman. Did you know he was from Missouri? And Billy Bones was very fond of him."

*Billy who?* I almost asked, but then my stomach growled again and I decided I would faint with hunger if I had to wait long enough to hear the answer. "So what about a cat, huh?"

"I don't know." She was wavering.

"We could just look."

"I'm not so sure—"

"Puh-lease," I whined.

"All right," Grandma surrendered reluctantly. "Sometime in the next few days, we'll visit the pound. If we happen to come across a fierce Missouri-looking cat, then maybe—"

It was near enough to victory. "Breakfast?" I interrupted.

"Oh, my." My grandmother clapped her hands. "I have some oatmeal on the stove. It's nothing fancy, but it will stick to your ribs until lunchtime."

I plastered a grateful smile on my face.

Grandma dished me up a bowl. I thought she would leave it at that, but she put a slice of butter on top and then covered it all with a heaping spoonful of brown sugar.

"Cream?" she asked.

"Yes'm."

She set the bowl down in front of me, along with a big glass of orange juice.

By the time I was done, I'd decided that Grandma's oatmeal covered in butter and brown sugar and cream was my second favorite breakfast meal, right behind eggs, sausages, and toast.

Of course, I wasn't about to give her the satisfaction of hearing me admit it.

# Chapter Seven

"It is a Craftsman-style house," she had announced proudly, beginning the tour of her house at the front door as soon as we'd cleaned up the breakfast dishes.

"Dad says Craftsman tools are the best," I said, with a yawn.

"I wouldn't know about that," Grandma replied softly, "but Craftsman is the name they use for this kind of house. I have owned it for nearly thirty years."

She pointed out the tiny panes that surrounded the big front windows. "Leaded glass," she said.

"Of course," I replied, peering closely at the glass and acting as if I knew what she was talking about.

When I looked up, she was already disappearing into the living room. I hurried after her, stepping into a room filled with big old wood furniture that was overflowing with so many fancy, colorful pillows, it was hard to see where anyone could find a place to sit. A gleaming black grand piano sat like a gigantic clam in one corner.

"Who plays that?"

"No one anymore," Grandma admitted. "I heard you are a talented piano player."

I shrugged.

"I suppose you will want to play," she sighed, "and that means I'd better get it tuned." She said it as if it was my fault she'd have to spend the money to have it tuned.

I drifted over to the piano and ran a finger up and down the keys. "Sounds good enough to me," I said, startled by the rich, full sounds that filled the room.

"But not to me," Grandma said sourly. "You can sharpen a pencil on that middle C. As soon as it is tuned, you can start playing it. Not before. Nothing is more up-setting than an out-of-tune piano."

I wondered what she'd say after a few more days of my anti-Grandma campaign. She was in no mood to daw-dle, and led me into a dining room large enough to house a massive rectangular wooden table that was darkened with age and gleaming from regular buffing. It was surrounded by the kind of chairs that King Arthur might have used at his Round Table. There was more of the big dark furniture against the walls, and a bay window that looked out over the backyard.

Grandma didn't waste any time there, either, pointing it all out with a wave of her arm. She marched back into the kitchen, gesturing with her chin at a door she said led to the basement. "Washer and dryer are down there," she explained. "I also store canned goods, rice, and bottles of water, jam, and such. That's where we'll go if those filthy, godless Communists decide to attack."

I gave her a sideways glance, figuring it was another screwball attempt at a joke. But the scowl on her face told me she was serious.

Maybe she really was crazy.

And then it was back upstairs. I already knew Mom's bedroom and the bathroom across the hallway. She pointed them out anyway. "And there's an extra bedroom and my room," she explained, rapping on two other wooden doors with her knuckles. "Towels and such are in the closet," she said, announcing the end of the tour.

"What about that one?" I pointed at the six-panel wooden door at the end of the hallway.

She shook her head. "It is nothing."

But I'd caught the faint catch in her voice, the way she pronounced that word, as if "nothing" was really everything in the whole world.

I was trying the doorknob before she had a chance to object. It was locked.

"Nothing worthwhile up there," Grandma hollered, "just an attic filled with junk, the kind of things I should have had hauled off and burned long ago. I always keep the door locked," she added. I'm sure it was just for my benefit.

As a kid growing up in apartments, I knew I'd missed out on a few things. Backyards, for one, where I could play and imagine and not have to share with anyone else. Those magical realms called attics were another.

I had always wanted to live in a house with an attic, and now I had the chance. I could already imagine exploring it on a rainy day or, better yet, turning it into a permanent hideout, a place where I could read and write letters to Dad without being interrupted.

I rattled the doorknob again, just for good measure. Just because I was hoping to leave soon didn't mean I couldn't sneak in sometime before that and take a look.

"It is always locked," Grandma intoned again, like a queen issuing a proclamation. She turned and headed back downstairs. "Come along, Maya."

"Okay, Grandma," I said, sweetly. A few years ago, Elizabeth's older brother had showed me a few tricks. I'd always figured he'd end up in prison, but he was in law school, learning some tricks of a different kind, I suppose. But thanks to him, I hadn't met a locked door yet that I couldn't get around.

*Piece of cake*, I said to myself.

# Chapter Eight

Grandma left the dishes, pots, and pans for me to do. All through dinner, she'd picked at her fried chicken leg and peas, and she'd barely touched her mashed potatoes. She fled upstairs as soon as I was done eating, complaining of a migraine headache, and announcing that we were going to skip Wednesday night church.

I almost felt sorry for her.

Almost.

No doubt "headache" was just another name for me.

Whatever the reason, I was happy to have her out of the way for a while. It gave me the perfect opportunity to do some snooping.

I hurried through the dishes without being asked. I left the frying pan soaking in warm soapy water and started exploring right away. I opened every drawer, cabinet, and closet I could find, looking into places I'd never have been brave enough to try if someone had been watching.

I didn't feel guilty about it. Not really.

It wasn't like I was reading her diary or pawing through hidden-away pictures, though I certainly searched high and low for anything that looked like a diary.

I was just, well, curious, that's all.

And there was something else—something I couldn't quite identify. It was almost as if I was being led from one room to the next. My past was a puzzle, but instead of the pieces being stored carefully in a box kept safely in a cupboard, they all had been scattered, one by one, all over the house.

In the basement, I came across stacks of long-forgotten books and boxes of ancient magazines, the most recent from October 1938. Nothing after that. Odd. I wondered . . . what had happened in 1938? Had Grandma just tired of magazines in the fall of 1938 and decided to quit reading them after that? Was it as simple as that? Or had something more serious—or even sinister—happened way back then?

My suspicions deepened when I came across a closet filled with men's suits, shirts, and coats. Was this another connection with 1938? They certainly looked old. And the smell of mothballs and ancient tobacco smoke that wafted out when I opened the closet door was so strong it made my eyes water. As I stepped back, I noticed hats that a gangster might have worn lining the top shelf.

Maybe leftover clothes from an ex-boyfriend? A gangster, even? Maybe he'd used the house as a hideout. The very idea was so hard to imagine it almost made me laugh out loud. Of course, there was an easier explanation. Grandpa. It was a strange word, one that I was not used to saying. Daddy was an orphan. He had never known his family, so I had no grandparents from him. But Grandma had been married once. I had a grandfather, but he died long before I was born. He was part of a past so distant that Mom never even talked about him.

After I was done exploring the basement and the main floor, I would still have the upstairs rooms and the attic to snoop in. The attic would have to wait for a time when Grandma wasn't around. No doubt she would hear any fiddling with the lock, unless she had a bottle hidden in her room and was too drunk to notice the noise. I was almost tempted to knock on her door and see if "migraine" was also another word for vodka, but I decided against it.

I finished up in the dining room. That was where I stayed the longest, staring at the checkerboard of framed black-and-white photographs on the wall. I recognized Mom in a few pictures and picked out my grandma in some others. She looked so young and happy that I almost didn't recognize her.

But most of the photos were of strangers. And yet, these people on the wall had something to do with my grandmother and my mom, meaning they also had something to do with me. In other words, some of them were *my* people. For some reason, that idea made my stomach flutter and the hair on the back of my neck stand up. I knew absolutely nothing about them. All my life, I'd had my mom and dad, and now there was this grandma that I hardly knew and didn't like much. Beyond that was a void that should have been filled by all those people on the wall—aunts and uncles, cousins, and grandparents. But it wasn't. They were still just the faces of strangers to me.

In the end, the *something* I was looking for that night remained vague, indistinct, and undiscovered, if it even existed at all. I fought back a yawn, glaring at the faces in warning—to any of their ghosts who might happen to be watching—that it was best to leave me alone. I remembered to lock the front door, turned off the downstairs lights, and trudged slowly upstairs.

Sleep didn't come easily that night. There were the usual reasons: I wasn't used to the bed, and the house seemed to come awake as soon as I slipped beneath the covers. It creaked and groaned like an old dog left outside all night. But the real reason I had trouble sleeping was because of all those unknown people on that wall downstairs.

I couldn't stop wondering who they were or what they had been like.

And I couldn't stop wondering what they might think of me.

# Chapter Nine

Harry S. Truman came home with us in a cardboard boot box the next afternoon. Not the dignified, respectful way you'd want to transport a former president of the United States, but perfectly suitable for a big yellow tabby with sharp claws and a bad temper.

Just my luck that Grandma would open the boot box that held Harry the cat right there in the dining room, under that wall of old family photographs. I had a hard time paying attention to the cat with all those strangers staring over my shoulder. But as soon as Grandma peeked under the lid and I heard Harry S. hiss at her in response, I forgot all about the pictures.

"Do you think we should let him out?" she asked.

"I don't see how keeping him cooped up in there is going to make him any friendlier," I said, pointing out what I thought was obvious.

"Yes, of course, that's true," Grandma said, carefully lifting the lid.

Harry S. was crouched in the center of the box, his legs quivering like loaded springs. He squinted and blinked at Grandma, his ears flat back against his skull, huge eyes green and sparkling like giant Life Savers. He glanced at me, spat, and then, realizing that nothing was stopping him, exploded out of the box. The last thing I saw was his back end scooting around the corner.

"I suppose we just need to give her some time," Grandma said, giving me a frank look. "She needs to satisfy herself that we are not as horrid as she might think. God's creatures are smart. Left alone, they can figure it out."

"Harry's a *he*," I reminded her.

"Yes, that's right," Grandma said, still eyeing me. "Until he settles down, I will need your help in keeping an eye on him."

I shrugged. I was feeling grumpy. This was not working out like I had hoped. Grandma had seemed to like visiting the pound. Something about seeing animals trapped in cages must be invigorating for people like her. Though we had been unlucky enough to find a cat that met her criteria for replacing Franklin D. Roosevelt, I hadn't expected her to take to him right away. Either there was something particularly appealing about Harry S. Truman that I wasn't able to see, or Grandma's affection for her recently departed feline was more bark than bite. I was kind of sorry I hadn't insisted on naming him Richard M. Nixon.

She stood up and brushed down the front of her dress. "Hungry?"

I shrugged again and followed her into the kitchen.

"Sit," was all she said, pointing at the table. I slid into the chair. A few moments later, she placed a big glass of milk in front of me and a thick slick of bread, slathered with blackberry jam. "This is last year's jam," she said. "We need to finish it up. We may be picking berries soon if we get a few weeks of hot weather."

She sat down across from me with a plate and some bread of her own. She cleared her throat and began talking instead of eating.

She started off by announcing that she was looking forward to a pleasant summer together.

The statement was so blatantly false I nearly choked on my bread. *Liar*, I almost muttered. I took another bite of bread instead.

She said she expected me to help out around the house, keep my room picked up and the bathroom straight, and chip in on doing the dishes.

I felt like waving my hand and interrupting, asking her if she thought I was some sort of bum or hippie or something. Of course I would do my part, at least until she sent me packing. But she didn't give me a chance. She went on for what felt like another ten minutes, lecturing me about my duties and responsibilities as a guest in her home. "This used to be a family neighborhood," she explained, "but the children have either grown up or the families have moved away. I don't know most of the people anymore. Oh, there is a Mexican family down the block. And Mrs. Garcia seems nice enough. But their children are all over the place. Everyone speaking Mexican. I suppose you might find someone your age there."

What did I care about making new friends and finding kids to "play" with? She made it sound like I was five years old or something. No, I wasn't going to be around long enough to need new friends.

She said she expected me to go with her to church on Wednesday nights and Sundays. "When times get tough," she said, "it is good to know you have a friend in Jesus."

"Uh-huh," I replied, wondering if she knew that her good friend Jesus had been dead for 2,000 years.

Of course, Mom had neglected to tell me about all the churchgoing I'd have to do. But one more thing wasn't going to make a difference. I couldn't get any angrier than I already was.

Grandma also explained how she worked part-time at the downtown library and that on those days, I would go with her to work. "I have taken this week off for your arrival. We will start first thing Monday."

I waved a hand. "Excuse me?"

"Yes, Maya."

"You said 'we will,' as in you and me."

"Yes."

"So I'm going with you to work?"

"You have something against libraries?"

I shook my head. "No, that's not it. I love the library. It's just—"

"Oh, don't worry, there are thousands and thousands of books to explore. You won't run out of things to do." She folded her hands on her lap. "Any more questions?"

I had a few, but none that she would be interested in hearing, and none that mattered too much, particularly since I would be leaving soon enough. Besides, going with her to the library would get me out of her house. She couldn't possibly watch me every moment at the library.

And that made me think about shopping downtown.

For that, I would need some extra money. I couldn't afford to waste the money I had "borrowed" from Mom.

"I was wondering about my allowance," I said, some angel whispering the suggestion in my ear.

"Pardon me?"

"Mom pays me an allowance," I said, making it up as

I went along, "for keeping my room picked up, the bathroom straightened up, and chipping in with doing the dishes."

"How much?"

"Seven dollars a week," I said. It was hard not to keep from bursting out laughing at my bald-faced lie, remembering what Mom had said when I asked about getting an allowance like the rest of my friends.

"No one pays me for cooking and cleaning," she had said. "Don't see why I should pay you for doing what's expected. You want some extra money of your own, you must do extras."

"Your mother and I did not discuss any allowance," my grandma said, "but I suppose I could afford seven dollars."

I was already thinking about what I could do with my allowance money, but my grandma kept going: "Of course, your room and board is a dollar a day. So instead of owing me seven dollars a week, I guess as long as you do your chores—to my satisfaction, that is—we are even."

"Room and board?"

"Why, yes," my grandma said, a faint smile on her lips. "You don't think I'm rich enough to let you stay in my house and eat my food for free, do you?"

I felt like I had just been mugged by a gang of old

ladies. I had gone from seven dollars a week richer to back where I started in less time than it takes to say how-dee-doo. And my nutball of a grandma had handled it so smoothly that I couldn't even get mad at her.

I was half tempted to call her bluff. She wasn't really charging me or my mom for letting me stay with her, was she? What grandmother would do such a thing?

On the other hand, I could already tell that she wasn't like other grandmothers I'd met. I'd seen the way she stiffed the cab driver out of his tip. And usually other grandmas weren't complete strangers like mine was.

"One last thing," she said. "I just want to say how sorry I am about your daddy. Lord knows he and I didn't see eye to eye—"

I jumped to my feet, sending my chair tumbling across the kitchen floor.

"There's nothing to be sorry about," I exploded, arms rigid by my side, hands clenched into white-knuckled fists. "He's just fine. I have letters from him. He's coming back. It's just a mix-up. I expect to hear about it any day now. And then I'll get to go back home, and I won't need to stay at this . . . this rotten old place with an old crow like you!"

The tears were already running down my face by the time I reached the first step, and I was full-blown blubbering when I threw myself onto my mom's bed and buried my face in the pillow.

A few hours later, there was a soft knock on the door. By now it was dark outside. I didn't care about missing dinner. I was sitting at my mom's old desk. I'd found paper and a pen in the drawer and was writing my dad a letter, telling him about what a fine time I was having in Seattle. I was lying to him because I didn't want him to worry about me. I wrote about the new cat. I knew he'd laugh when he read about a cat named after a president. Dad loved to laugh more than anyone I knew.

"What?" I said, reaching forward and turning up my transistor radio, hoping the angry snarl of Jimi Hendrix's guitar would give Grandma the message that I was in no mood to be bothered, particularly by her.

"May I come in for a moment?"

*It's your house*, I thought, but I kept quiet, hoping she would go away and leave me alone.

She didn't. I heard her step into the room all right, but she stayed by the door, so I kept working on my letter, bobbing my head to Jimi's solo, acting like I didn't know she was there.

If she was waiting for an apology, she was going to stand there a long time. In fact, I almost hoped she'd start yelling at me. That would have made me feel better. Or maybe she'd announce that she was sending me back home. That would have eased the knot in my stomach and solved all my problems.

Instead, she said, "Can I get you anything?"

"I'm fine," I said.

"Are you?"

I didn't say anything. I didn't turn around, even though the way she said those words made it sound like she actually cared.

I heard her turn to go. "There is one thing," I said tonelessly, stopping her in the doorway.

"What's that?"

"Envelopes and stamps. I didn't bring any with me."

"I have some you can use in the rolltop desk downstairs."

"How much will they cost?"

"Nothing. Use as many as you like."

"I'd rather buy my own."

A pause before she responded. "The closest place is Guy's, a few blocks away. I can take you there later."

"Fine," I said.

"Maya, about your father—"

"He's doing just fine," I snapped. "You'll all see. He's just great! He's better than ever! And he's coming home soon!"

The pause was longer this time. "I left a plate of food in the refrigerator for you," she said.

I heard the door close, and she was gone.

# Chapter Ten

"How are you this beautiful Seattle morning?" Grandma said, greeting me as if nothing was wrong as I walked into the kitchen.

I gave her a wary look. "Okay, I guess. Hungry."

"That's how it should be for a growing young woman. I hope you don't mind having oatmeal again."

"No, I guess not." *She's a sneaky one*, I thought, almost admiring her sudden change in tactics. It was as if one of my enemies at school, someone I couldn't pass in the hallway without holding my nose, had suddenly decided to be nice to me.

I was in no mood for arguing about my dad, so we ate breakfast in icy silence, broken only by the occasional question from my grandma. I answered with wary, one-syllable responses: "Yeah," "No," "Sure," or "Uh-huh."

When I was about done with my oatmeal, Grandma announced that she had gardening to do. "Would you like to help?" she asked, making it sound like it was an invitation to an ice cream parlor.

I thought about responding with something like "Oh, boy, gardening, that's what I've always wanted to do!"

But I didn't feel like fighting. I just wanted everything to be the way it used to be.

I wanted to be back home.

I wanted Mom happy again.

And most of all, I wanted to look up and see my dad reading the sports section. He'd take a sip of coffee, see me eyeing him, and then give me a wink. "How about a ball game this afternoon, Honey Bear?"

But wanting doesn't make it so. I was here, Mom was by herself in San Francisco, and Dad was somewhere in South Vietnam.

"Think the Orioles have a chance this year?" I asked.

"You can't find any orioles out here," Grandma sputtered, eyeing me quizzically. "They are an eastern bird, I do believe."

"Never mind," I said, wondering why I had even bothered to ask her about baseball. "I have a few letters to write. Maybe you can give me directions to that store and I can go there instead."

Grandma thought for a moment and then nodded her assent. "I suppose you are old enough to go alone. I'll give you a list. You can pick up a few items for me, too."

She grunted to her feet and announced loudly that she would do the dishes, fishing, I suppose, for an "attagirl" from me. When I didn't bite, she grumped, "Have you seen Harry S. Truman?"

"Nope," I said, setting my bowl and spoon in the sink. I had heard him prowling the hallway outside my room during the night. He was probably off sleeping somewhere right at that moment.

"There was a window open in the dining room," she said. "He may have jumped outside. I hope he hasn't run off. Animals can find their way home, you know, but who knows where home used to be for him?"

That gave me a goofy thought. What if Harry was a San Francisco cat? Suppose someone had moved to Seattle from San Francisco and Harry had run away. But home was so far away, he couldn't figure out the best way to get started. Maybe he was prowling the waterfront, looking for the next boat to San Fran. The bigger deal, I suppose, was that he no longer had any home to go back to. Dumb, stupid cat.

"So why don't you see if he is hiding somewhere in the backyard?" Grandma suggested. "He hasn't had breakfast yet. We have no cat food yet, but I have never met a cat that doesn't like milk. Let's set some out on the back porch."

"Sure," I said, feeling a flush of worry on the back of my neck, imagining how Harry must feel, all by himself in a new place.

I banged my way out the back door, called out loudly, "Harry!" and then realized how stupid it was before I said it again. No self-respecting cat ever responded to a call. Dogs, of course, would respond to just about anything, but cats were different, more self-possessed and sure of themselves, less needy. Even if he was confused about his identity, thinking he was more dog than cat, he would probably still consider himself Waldo or Fluffy or whatever name his previous owners had used, so he'd probably just ignore my calls anyway.

Of course, Harry was no dummy. I found him a few minutes later, lying in the cool damp dirt beneath one of my grandma's azalea bushes, surveying the backyard like he already owned it. No doubt he had recognized a good deal right off. Nice house, regular food, no fresh little kids to bother him. Rodent-hunting safaris whenever he was bored. It was perfect. Why would he go anywhere else?

He watched me approach, staring me right in the face with those unblinking cat eyes, not bothering to get up and run off. I suppose he realized that I was about as much of a threat as a ladybug.

I sat down cross-legged on the grass next to him and

began scratching him between the eyes. When he moved his head, I went to work on his ear. That's when his purr motor turned on and I knew he didn't hate me. The way he'd acted coming out of the boot box had been just that—an act.

Sitting there in the tree-filtered sunshine, scratching Harry S.'s ears, I had my first real chance to inspect my grandmother's backyard.

I had to admit I liked it right off—not that I was an expert in backyards. A weathered fence, gray boards crowded tightly together, defined the boundaries. Big trees—maples, I learned later on—stood guard on either side of the yard, their long, thick branches extending like the necks of greedy hatchlings. Huge leaves filtered the sunlight like the panes of a stained glass window, making everything glow with greens and yellows.

In the quiet, I could sense the pulse of my own throbbing heart. In the distance, I could hear the faint roar of traffic from the freeway, a distant chattering jackhammer, the wail of a siren, all joining in a symphony of sound. But it seemed far away and didn't intrude on the peace of this place.

I took a deep breath, relaxing for the first time in days. I let my eyes wander over to the house next door—at least, the part of it I could see above the fence.

I always noticed everything. Dad said I could pick out a freckle on the face of a mosquito at twenty paces.

Even so, I almost missed the freckles on the boy's face. Something about the still, robot-like way he stood there, framed by the second-story window, almost fooled me into thinking he was a statue instead of someone alive and breathing.

"What the—" I sputtered. I shaded my eyes with my hand to get a better look. He had pale white skin the color of bleached flour and a head of brown hair that hung down thickly over his forehead. He wore a shirt and a sweater. He looked about my age, though it was hard to be sure.

But then he began rocking back and forth. At first, I suspected that his rocking was a goofy way of making fun of me. As I continued to watch him, I realized that he wasn't seeing me at all.

I grabbed Harry S., draped him over my shoulder, and headed for the house, all the while keeping an eye on the strange boy. Grandma's yard might be nice, but I wasn't particularly keen about living next door to someone who might be a little crazy.

At the back door, I paused and gave the boy one last look, still not completely convinced he wasn't playing some weird joke on me.

I waved, just to see what would happen. For a moment, I almost thought he noticed. He stopped rocking for just a beat or two. I could have sworn that his eyes focused on me. But then, before he had a chance to wave back, a pair of hands pulled him away from the window.

## Chapter Eleven

"I wouldn't know," Grandma said a little while later, her little garden shovel pausing in the air as she considered my question, then diving back into the rich, brownie-colored soil.

"Kid about my age. White boy. Brown hair—"

Grandma pursed her lips. "Ahh, yes. They are new. Noticed the moving van out front a week or two ago, blocking the sidewalk as if they owned it, in fact. So I told those movers I was going to call the city if they did not get it out of the way. Of all the rude, impertinent . . . "

"What did they do?" I interrupted.

"They moved it," Grandma said, like there had never been any doubt. She dug out two more quick scoops of dirt, then slipped a petunia into the hole. "It'll have purple flowers."

I knew what she was getting at. Purple was my favorite color, and normally, I would have said something polite. But I was more interested in the kid next door. "Well, whatever his name is," I said, "he gave me the creeps. Rocking back and forth, staring at nothing at all, and then these hands came out of nowhere and yanked him out of sight. I wonder if they're. . . " I paused and gave Grandma a sideways look. "Communists."

She didn't bite. Instead, she shook her head with disapproval. "You know absolutely nothing about that boy and his family, and you're already making judgments about them."

That wasn't exactly true. I already knew one important thing: that boy next door was a human metronome. "Okay, then, I think we should find out more about him," I said.

"I think we mind our own business," she snapped. "Besides, they're—"

"White?" I interrupted.

Grandma waved her hand in the air like she was shooing away a fly, but I noticed she didn't disagree with me. "The word I was going to use was *English*."

"As in England English?"

Grandma nodded. She finished planting the last of the petunias and then dabbed her forehead with a pink hanky. "Enough for today. Time for me to put my feet up for a bit. Do you need anything?"

I shook my head.

"I thought you were going to get some envelopes and stamps?"

"Later," I said.

"Suit yourself," Grandma said, with an indifferent shrug. I watched her creak to her feet and make her way back into the house.

Twenty minutes later, I snuck inside. Grandma had her feet up all right, propped on the stool in front of the big soft chair in the living room. She was asleep, her mouth open slightly, faint snores hissing from her lips.

I crept back into the kitchen, flicked on the oven, and started to work.

The first time I made cookies on my own, I was only five years old. When I pulled the pan out of the oven and tried one, I thought it tasted like an old sponge and started to cry. "Forgot the sugar," my mom said, taking a nibble from one and making a face.

My dad, however, swore they were the best ever. He ate nearly every one, and then he helped me make another batch. And that time, we didn't forget the sugar.

Today, I worked quietly, mixing the flour and eggs in a plastic bowl. After some searching, I found chocolate chips in a drawer beside the refrigerator and sprinkled some into the dough. Of course, a few managed to find their way into my mouth while I worked.

As I began to line up little balls of dough in rows on the greased pan, I also slipped a few chunks into my mouth. Anyone who has ever made cookies knows that sampling the dough is the best part. My friend Elizabeth and I often made cookies just so we could eat the cookie dough, washing it down with tall glasses of cold milk, eating and drinking until we were about to burst.

I slid the pan into the oven. Before long, the kitchen filled with the most delicious smell. Even Harry S. seemed to like it. He began weaving through my legs, occasionally stopping to rub his whiskers on the corner of the doorway and the edge of the stove.

"My, my, you are the little worker," Grandma said from the doorway as I finished stacking a dozen cookies on a plate. "What is the occasion?" She yawned into her hand.

I grabbed the plate and held it out to her.

"Mmmmm. Tastes as good as it smells," she said, nibbling the corner of a cookie. "I didn't think girls cooked anymore."

"I'm an exception," I said.

"I can see that," Grandma remarked.

Before she could ask another question, I grabbed her by the hand and pulled her toward the door. Cookies were only half of my plan.

"Where are we going?"

I had to drop her hand to open the door, but I picked it up again as soon as we were outside. I dragged her across the lawn to the house next door and pulled her up the steps. Before she had a chance to squeak, complain, or run away, I kicked on the door with my right foot.

"I thought it might be nice to meet that kid, Rocky, and his parents," I said, with a malicious grin.

A slight, pale-faced woman wearing a long gypsy skirt and an oversized T-shirt peered cautiously around the door. "Yes?" she said.

Grandma glared daggers in my direction and then stretched her face into something close to a friendly smile, deciding, at that moment, I suppose, to make the best of the situation.

"My name is Ruby St. Clair," my grandma announced. "I live next door."

"Yes?" the woman repeated, not bothering to open the door wider or invite us in.

"And this is my granddaughter, Maya. She just arrived the other day from San Francisco."

"Hi," I said, with a wave, trying to peer around the woman and see if I could spot that kid inside the house.

"We're sorry to bother you," said Grandma, squeezing my hand tight as she said those words, her way of saying

I'd be sorry as soon as she got me back home. "My grand-daughter thought it was high time to stop by for a wel-coming visit. I don't know how it is where you come from, but it is a custom here."

"Oh, I see," the woman said, plucking nervously at the front of her T-shirt.

She still made no effort to respond to our neighborly gesture. In fact, this lady was beginning to make me mad. I had just gone to all the trouble of making cookies for her and that strange kid, and I was even hand delivering them, but here she was, treating us like we were selling vacuum cleaners. I didn't know if she was just rude or if that was how people from England acted.

She ran a hand through her hair and finally smiled. "I'm sorry. My name is Petula. Petula Richards. I'd invite you in, it's just—"

At that moment, a howl burst out from inside the house. It rolled over us like a clap of thunder, and I imag-ined some huge, demented dog, its fangs slashing this way and that, ready to leap on us the moment we turned to run.

I didn't care. I was ready to leave the cookies on the steps and split, experiment over.

Grandma, however, had other ideas. She lowered her shoulder, pushed past Mrs. Richards, and barged into the house, dragging me along with her. Since we'd already come that far, she just wanted to see it through, I suppose.

Or maybe she was just curious.

"We'll leave these on the table," Grandma said, looking around.

Instead of monsters, demons, or demented dogs, there was just that same strange boy. He was sitting at the big wooden dining table, all calm and quiet-like. In his hand was a bright red crayon. He was holding it up to the light streaming through the front window, studying it as if it were the most amazing thing in the entire world. The only other hint that things might not be normal—besides the howl a few moments earlier, that is—was the jumble of papers and crayons scattered everywhere.

"You must think me so inhospitable," stammered Mrs. Richards apologetically, brushing back her hair. "The house is a disaster, and Tommy, well, he's having some difficulties adjusting to all the changes since we moved here."

"Change can be hard for anyone," Grandma said, glancing in my direction.

"He's, he's a special child," Mrs. Richards said.

*Special* wasn't a word I would have used. *Goofy*, *freaky*, *weird*, and *whacked* were just a few that came to my mind. But I decided to keep them to myself. "Wanna cookie?" I said. "They're almost as good as the dough."

Mrs. Richards gave me a distracted smile. "How kind."

I took a few steps forward and stuck the plate under Tommy's nose. Any regular kid would have started drooling right then and there. But that Tommy was a superman. He didn't even wrinkle his nose. I couldn't help but be impressed by his self-control.

"We'll just leave them here," Grandma added, shaking her head in my direction. "You can return the plate anytime."

Mrs. Richards nodded. She was opening and closing her mouth, as if she had more to say but wasn't quite sure how to start.

"Go ahead," I said. "We won't bite, you know."

Mrs. Richards sighed. "It's just, well, Tommy, you see, is one of the reasons we decided to come here—for help. We're participating in a special program this summer at the medical center. My husband and I are both very optimistic. . . ."

She didn't sound that way to me. As her voice trailed off, I noticed with sudden alarm that Grandma was nodding her head as if she knew exactly what it was like to have a son who howled like a mad dog.

"Anything we can do to ease your burdens," my grandma said, "you make sure to let us know."

*We? Us? Why was I included?* Even worse, she'd made the offer without even checking with me.

"You're too kind, Mrs. St. Clair, but you don't know what you're offering."

"That's true," I chimed in, hoping Grandma would reconsider, hoping to get my little stunt back under control and Grandma out the door.

Grandma shrugged away my hand. "Maybe it will help if you tell us a little more about your family."

Mrs. Richards gave her a suspicious look that softened as soon as she realized that Grandma really was interested.

"This has been fun," I interrupted, "but I think we should be going. Harry S., yes, that's right, he's probably worrying about us."

"Hush, Maya. We have plenty of time, and I doubt that cat has even noticed that we are gone."

Mrs. Richards led us into her living room. She sat in a straight-backed chair by the window. Grandma and I shared the couch.

"I'm sorry," she said, as soon as we were comfortable. "You see, Tommy has a disorder."

"You mean, he's autistic?" Grandma interrupted.

"Why, quite right," Mrs. Richards said, surprised.

"I know a little about it," Grandma explained. "Please go on."

"Oh, yes, well, as you know, autism means that it is

difficult for him to interact with people and objects. He doesn't read, write, or laugh. He knows just a few words. I've never even heard him say *Mummy*. Not once. My word, I'm not even sure he knows what I am, let alone who I am. Can you imagine what it's like? The only thing that seems to help—that he seems to truly enjoy—is music."

"You don't say?" Grandma said, glancing around the room. "Too bad you don't have a piano he can bang around on."

Mrs. Richards gave her head a shake, her cheeks growing red with emotion. "We had one in England. My mother's, actually. She gave it to us a few months ago, and he took to it like he'd always played it. You can't imagine the difference it made for Tommy."

Grandma, glancing at Tommy and then back at Mrs. Richards, replied, "Well, isn't that nice."

To me, it was pretty obvious what Grandma was thinking. I figured it was probably the same thing I was thinking. "Yeah, right."

"We were promised a piano but, as you can bloody well see—" Mrs. Richards threw up her hands. "I didn't realize how much Tommy would miss it . . . how much *I* would miss it."

Whoa. It was suddenly as clear to me as the glasses on Elizabeth's nose where this was heading.

"You aren't a Communist, are you?" I blurted out,

hoping she would confess right then and there, halting the direction this conversation was going.

"Pardon?"

"Communist," I repeated.

"Maya!" Grandma interjected sharply.

Mrs. Richards gave a loud belly laugh, her mood suddenly brightening. She leaned back in her chair, waving her hands in my direction. "Oh, it's quite all right. Isn't everyone a Communist at one time or another? I was one for a few months in college, but it was only because this boy was a Communist and I thought he was cute. When he asked out my best friend instead of me, I decided Communism wasn't my cup of tea. I did vote for the Labor Party in the last election, though, in case you're curious."

I could tell by the smile on Grandma's face that she was satisfied by that explanation. She'd probably been a Communist, too, when she was younger.

"I have a piano," Grandma said, before I could squawk an objection. "I would be more than happy to let Tommy play it. I work three mornings a week—Monday, Wednesday, and Friday. Sunday we're at church. Just let me know when it might be convenient for you to bring Tommy over. Perhaps we can visit while he's playing."

Mrs. Richards acted as if she had just won a lottery. She jumped up from her chair, grasped Grandma's hands, gave her a quick hug, and then stepped back, embarrassed, I suppose, by the sudden display of emotion.

When I glanced over at Tommy in the dining room, he was still staring at the crayon as if it were a precious jewel. But I noticed that his eyes kept flickering over at us and then back to his crayon. I also noticed that every time someone said "piano," his feet twitched like someone was tickling him with a feather.

"Piano!" I yelled.

Sure enough, his feet began to jerk up and down.

"Maya?" Grandma said.

"I was so super excited, I just had to let out a shout," I said, my voice dripping with sarcasm.

"How charming," Mrs. Richards said, giving me a warm smile. Grandma, however, was back to looking at me as if I were a bug from Mars. "It's time for us to go," she announced.

"See ya, Rocky," I said, pinching Tommy on the arm as I walked by. He didn't even respond. *You may have fooled them*, I thought, *but you haven't fooled me.*

# Chapter Twelve

Mrs. Richards and Tommy came over for a visit the next afternoon.

Gray. That was a word for the day. It suited my mood. The sky was a swollen blanket that seemed to hang a few feet above the rooftops. A blustery wind was blowing in off Elliott Bay, racing up the hill, and flinging sheets of rain at Grandma's house in a way that made me wonder if we had been magically transported to the inside of a car wash.

It seemed like January, not the third week in June.

I had a head cold and was wrapped up in a sweater and a blanket, sitting on the couch surrounded by a snow-drift of used tissues and crumpled stationery. I was work-ing on another letter to Dad, relaying an account of the previous day and my speculations about the English boy, Tommy.

I wanted to write to him about how my strategy for

disrupting Grandma's life wasn't working the way I intended. Everything I suggested and did seemed to be having the opposite effect. Instead of hating Harry, Grandma actually seemed to like him. Instead of being mad that I had forced her to meet the people next door, she was becoming friends with Mrs. Richards. And I was in danger of being stuck with a nutball for a companion.

The only thing that hadn't changed was how I felt about being here. The sooner I was on my way back home, the better.

As for Grandma and me, we had settled into an edgy truce, like strange dogs sharing a yard. I was civil enough, and so was she. But other than specific questions or requests—Where's more toilet paper? Can I make a peanut butter and jelly sandwich? Please pass the butter—I didn't communicate with her, and she'd given up asking me questions. In other words, we occupied the same house, but that was about the extent of what we shared. I could only hope that it would be just a matter of time before it all came crashing down.

I heard Grandma answer the door and then usher Mrs. Richards inside. There was a rush of cold air on the back of my neck that made me shiver. Summer weather in San Francisco was never anything to brag about, so I guess I shouldn't have been surprised by Seattle's cold and rain.

It didn't help that at that moment, my head felt like a bicycle tube about to explode and my nose was clogged with a strange, glue-like gunk. My lips were swollen and cracked from constantly breathing through my mouth, making me look like I had just trekked across the Gobi Desert. Swabbing my lips with Vaseline had helped little. And adding insult to injury, my ears were so plugged up that I was having trouble overhearing what Grandma and Mrs. Richards were saying.

I did manage to pick out something about Mrs. Richards teaching a class on Shakespeare most weekday mornings. Then I heard "appointments for Tommy." Grandma mumbled a response. Right about then, my ears popped. It felt so wonderful that I almost sighed out loud. Then I very clearly heard Mrs. Richards say, "Wonderful!" followed by Grandma's reply, "That will work out just fine. Maya can use a new friend."

Whoa. Friend? Was she serious? That kid was a sneaky weirdo, plain and simple. There was no way in the world I would ever be caught dead calling Tommy my friend.

*Foe*, on the other hand, was a word that I was more comfortable using.

*Fee, fie, foe, fum, I smell the blood of an Englishman.*

As those words began to run through my head, I realized I might need to rethink my hatred of the giant in "Jack and the Beanstalk." What if we had it all wrong? We were supposed to be impressed by Jack's exploits, but in fact, he was a thief and an intruder, invading the giant's house, stealing the gold-laying hen, and who knows what else.

But I was too sick to object. So I contented myself with keeping an eye on Tommy as he wandered into the living room, sat down on the stool, lifted the keyboard cover, and then began fooling around on the piano. Grandma and Mrs. Richards drifted into the room and settled into a couple of big soft chairs near the piano.

Much to my disappointment, they seemed to take only about thirty seconds before they were fast friends, laughing and giggling like Elizabeth and me when we were together.

I wondered if they even knew what a weird pair they made.

In one corner, Mrs. Richards—"just call me Petula"— a teacher of Shakespeare and mom to the strangest kid I had ever met. With pale blue eyes and blonde hair that hung to her shoulders, she had, next to Tommy, the whitest skin I had ever seen. Though she was dressed like a hippie in a loose floral-print skirt and white blouse, she talked and carried herself like the Queen of England.

In the other corner, the great-granddaughter of a couple of slaves (or so the story goes), my neatly dressed, black-skinned, prim and proper, churchgoing grandmother. As far as I knew, she'd never gone to college, and she had grown up about as far from England as you could get—on a poor farm in the South.

I suppose what surprised me then, even more than their apparent quick friendship, was listening to Grandma talk. It made me forget all about Tommy and the piano.

College or not, I realized that Grandma was smart—scary smart. When Mrs. Richards mentioned a book, Grandma would begin nodding that she'd read it. I figured she was just faking it. That's what I would have done: *Uh-huh. Of course. Delightful.*

But guess what? She wasn't faking it. She told Mrs. Richards what she didn't like about the book, where she disagreed with the author, and how she didn't think this or that character was believable. At that moment, I realized I had seriously underestimated this strange new grandmother.

And I'd see Mrs. Richards nodding. But she wasn't nodding in that know-it-all way that smart people do when they think you aren't as smart as they are, but in a respectful, thoughtful way—one smart person to another. In fact, I could tell she was thinking hard about what

Grandma was saying. Maybe that is just about the best compliment one person can give to another.

That freak Tommy was another surprise.

I expected him to bang away on the keyboard like some stinky, diaper-wearing two-year-old.

Instead, I was shocked to hear him play like he had been taking lessons for years. Almost the first thing, his noodling turned into arpeggios, his fingers racing up and down the keys. Playing arpeggios was what I did to warm up for my lessons with Mrs. Friermuth. Arpeggios are just finger exercises, but it's hard to make them fast and smooth. And Tommy was a master at both.

And then he surprised me even more by beginning to play a song. It was one I didn't recognize, but I noticed Grandma's head jerk like she'd been hit by a jolt of electricity.

"My word," she exclaimed. "He's playing Nat King Cole—like an angel."

Mrs. Richards shook her head and smiled cynically. "I wish God would have been a little more evenhanded," she said in that dry, formal way that English people talk.

"What do you mean?" Grandma asked.

Mrs. Richards took a sip and then set her cup back in the saucer. "You won't believe me."

Grandma raised her eyebrows in a way that said "Try me."

Mrs. Richards gave an embarrassed wave of her hands. "Oh, dear. I suppose it can't hurt anything to admit it, so here it is: he just started playing the piano a few months ago."

"What?" I screeched, dropping my book on the floor.

"I know. Amazing, isn't it? It all started when I was playing a record. I don't know. They can't really explain it. And Tommy isn't the first autistic child to do this. In any case, who knows, something in his brain may have clicked. He just walked over to our piano, and after a few minutes of randomly pecking at the keys, he started playing back the song we had just been listening to—note for note. I tried another song, and the same thing happened. It went on like that for three hours. He can hear something once on the radio or the record player and play it back almost perfectly on the first go."

"I don't believe it," I muttered under my breath. I had practiced for years and years, and now this kid was playing piano way better than me after only a few months.

It wasn't fair. And it wasn't normal.

I peered more closely at Mrs. Richards. There was something unusual—something almost *alien*—about the color of her skin.

Right at that moment, Tommy began to play the theme music from one of my favorite TV shows, *The Twi-*

*light Zone.* The hair on the back of my neck stood up, and my mind raced. Maybe they weren't from London, England, but London, Mars, or maybe London, Venus? Maybe Tommy wasn't human at all, but—

"A gift from God," Grandma said, glaring briefly in my direction.

Mrs. Richards leaned forward in her chair. "Odd that you should say that. I thought the very same thing, too. But I'd trade it all for a boy who was a little more like, well, other boys. Isn't that a terrible thing for a mother to say?"

Even from my perch on the sofa, I could see her eyes glittering with tears. But she didn't cry. I could admire that.

Grandma didn't say anything. Her head was bowed, her eyes closed. She looked asleep.

I half expected her to embarrass me by breaking into prayer, waving her hands, and beseeching Jesus to intervene and save this poor child from the demons that afflicted him.

Instead, she opened her eyes, smiled in the saddest possible way, and then reached over and grabbed Mrs. Richards's hand. "It's not your fault, honey," Grandma said.

Mrs. Richards tried to smile, but faltered. I saw her chin tremble.

"We'll be back in a minute," Grandma said. "Keep him safe."

I watched them disappear down the hallway, not entirely understanding what was going on, but knowing enough to keep my mouth shut.

And through it all, Tommy kept playing. Now he was on to more modern music, leaving Nat King Cole behind and dabbling with the Beatles. I recognized the song: "Yesterday."

Of course, I wasn't fooled. In fact, as I listened, I grew even more convinced that his rocking, screeching, and not talking was just an act. It probably helped him get out of doing things he didn't want to do. I bet he never had to take out the garbage, do the dishes, clean his room, do homework, or go to bed on time. There were a thousand things a kid could avoid if he or she was a good actor.

And I was sure Tommy had found a way. If it was true—if he really was a big faker and not an alien kid from some faraway planet—it was a stroke of genius even I had to admire.

I had to give that Tommy credit; he was even sneakier than I had imagined.

# Chapter Thirteen

The next morning, I made the mistake of letting Grandma know I was feeling better, before I understood the consequences.

"Wonderful," she said. "The pastor is anxious to meet you."

"Pastor?"

"At my church."

"Church?"

"It is Sunday morning, Maya," she said, as if that was the only answer I needed. Apparently she didn't know that the only time I'd ever set foot in a church was the time my dad was lost. He had stopped at a small country church north of San Francisco to see if somebody inside could point us in the right direction. The way they'd reacted, you'd have thought we were the first blacks ever to visit. Who knows? Maybe we were.

"But, Grandma—"

"Yes?"

I tried to remember the word. I'd heard one of Mom's friends use it. Then it came to me. "I'm an atheist."

Grandma paused and stared at me. "And what do you think that means?" she said after a moment, her eyes glittering. I could almost hear her thinking, "Aha, you little snipe. I've got you now."

But not only had I remembered the word, I'd also remembered what it meant. *Got you now*, I thought. "It means I don't believe in God, Allah, Krishna, Buddha, or any other so-called Supreme Being," I said.

At first, Grandma winced as if I had just linked together a string of cusswords that would make even the most blue-tongued God hater proud. I was fairly confident that I had just taken care of all this church nonsense for the rest of my stay.

But then, to my utter horror, her wince transformed into a chuckle. The chuckle grew into a belly laugh, and before I knew it, she was laughing so hard, she had tears streaming down her face. I sat there watching it all, getting madder and madder, but uncertain what to do next.

When she finally regained control of herself, she stood up straight, put one hand on her right hip and said, "Honey, you can be whatever you want to be five and a half days a week. But when you are staying in my house, eating my food, and drinking my milk, it means every Sunday and Wednesday night, you are a Christian child. We are leaving in ten minutes. Any questions?"

I just stood there, mouth open, too stunned to stay mad or do anything.

"Any questions?" she repeated.

"I . . . I guess not," I stammered.

"Good." She glanced at her watch. "Now you have nine minutes."

I dashed upstairs to change out of my pajamas. What else could I do?

The Mt. Zion Holy Baptist Tabernacle and Church of God. That's the name of the church where Grandma had been going since my mom was a little girl. As we marched up the steps and through the front door, I fought back an impulse to grab her arm and hang on.

"Mornin', Miz St. Clair."

"Nice to see you, Ruby."

"And who's your young guest this mornin'?"

The greetings rained down on us like autumn leaves. I pasted a scowl of warning on my face and did my best to follow along in my grandma's wake.

As we stepped into the auditorium, I realized it was filled with more black people than I thought lived in all of Seattle. In fact, this place was filled with more black people than I had ever seen anywhere gathered in one place at the same time. Where had they all been hiding?

As I scanned the crowd, I noticed that all the men were dressed in fine-looking suits and that the shoes that were visible along the aisles were all polished to a new-car sheen.

But that was nothing compared to the women. Many of them looked like ancient African queens, wearing colorful dresses that poofed and billowed like bright flags, all topped off with the most ornate-looking hats I had ever seen.

Of course, as we made our way to our seats right in front, all Grandma's friends wanted to hug and pinch me. I must confess I didn't mind—not too much, anyway. They were so beautiful and sweet-smelling, it was like being hugged by flowers.

I flopped down onto my seat, expecting Grandma to join me. She didn't, but instead shrugged out of her coat, folded it neatly beside me, and placed her purse and hat on top. "I sing in the choir," she explained.

"What?"

"I'll be right up there," she said, gesturing over her shoulder. "Mrs. Davis, here, can keep you company."

"Hello, honey," rumbled the biggest woman I had ever seen. And I'm not talking fat, though she could have stood to lose a few pounds. There was only one word for it. She was HUGE. Everything about her was, well, big. Big orange hat, dress the size of a family tent, big orange earrings, and a pair of the biggest high-heeled orange dress shoes. They weren't just special order; they had to be one of a kind. Normally, I would have been alarmed by the sheer size of that woman, afraid that if she sneezed I might get crushed against the side of the pew, except for one thing. She also had the biggest, sweetest smile I had ever seen. It was so powerful, I could almost feel its warmth.

"Pleased to meet you, ma'am," I said, offering her my hand and a grin in return.

"What a polite child," she said, squeezing my hand lightly. "We'll get along just fine."

As I settled into my seat, reassured by the immense bulk of Mrs. Davis on my right, I didn't realize that all of this was just an appetizer.

I always figured that most churches—and by that I meant white churches—were solemn, serious, mind-fogging, soul-numbing places. They sang songs that were so sad and boring that just hearing them made you want to cover your ears and cry out in pain.

Elizabeth, who had been dragged to more services than I could count, said the sermons were usually even worse. Most of the preachers went on and on about what

a rotten person you were and how you'd better repent before it was too late—turn or burn, in other words—or else
they hustled you for money to finance yet another stained
glass window or a new Mercedes or Cadillac. I suppose I
might have thought the same thing if I had been hauled off
to church every Sunday when there were better things to
do, like watch the morning baseball game or laze away the
morning in bed with a good book.

But the Reverend Dr. Delbert R. Gillespie of the Mt.
Zion Holy Baptist Tabernacle and Church of God was no
hustler. From the opening words of his sermon, the cadence of his voice was pure scat, and his words were often
followed up with a riff of exclamation from three musicians on the right side of the stage, playing a drum set,
electric guitar, and organ—just to make sure you didn't
miss the point.

I confess, he never did quite make a Christian out of
me, but halfway through that first sermon, I understood
that he had a gift for making everyone feel better about
themselves. For as long as that congregation was under the
spell of his voice, they were committed to doing good—
me included. And there's nothing wrong with that.

But the high point of my first visit to church was not
Reverend Gillespie. It was the music. In fact, the choir was
so wild and joyous, so unchurch-like, I had trouble staying

in my seat when they started singing. That music had more in common with Motown than with church. In fact, I half expected to see Marvin Gaye dash out on stage and join in the fun.

Despite all the voices in that choir, I'm proud to say that Grandma's stood out over all the others. She sang like someone who performed regularly on the radio or *The Ed Sullivan Show*. Everyone in the choir seemed to like her voice, too. When she was singing, they'd turn to hear her better, with joyful smiles lighting up their faces.

Fortunately, not being able to stay in my seat wasn't a problem. Most of the time, when the choir was belting out a song, everybody was on their feet, swaying and clapping and yelling "Amen," and, occasionally, even dancing in the aisle.

I have to confess that before the sermon was over, I threw in a few shouts of my own. Sometimes it feels good to just yell. Fortunately, Mrs. Davis didn't seem to mind.

I said a few prayers for my dad, too. I figured I might as well cover all the bases.

# Chapter Fourteen

On Monday morning, we left the house precisely at 8:20 A.M., letting gravity pull our legs downhill.

My grandma worked three mornings a week at the main branch of the Seattle Library. And because she didn't want to leave me alone—after all, that was the main reason my mom sent me away for the summer—I was forced to go along.

Before we left the house, Grandma grabbed an umbrella from the big oak coat rack standing by the door. I thought about pointing out the bright, warm sunshine that spilled through the open door and across the floor, but I kept silent. No sense arguing with someone who expected the worst.

I guess one of the reasons I didn't put up more of a fuss about going to the library was because I actually liked libraries. Maybe it came from spending all that time with my mom at the college library when she was there studying. Libraries felt like a second home to me. In fact, my strongest and earliest memories are about the library. Dad used to chuckle that he wondered if I was born in a library. Mom would get red and shush him. But I sometimes thought maybe he wasn't kidding.

Whatever the reason, the smell of well-aged books, combined with the faint, almost imperceptible hum that I had decided long ago must come from all those eyeballs flitting back and forth across all those pages, had come to remind me of a friendly beehive and home.

It was an easy twenty-five-minute walk downhill. Grandma did most of the talking, prattling on about her work and her friends at the library. After a while, she began to sound like a whistling teakettle, droning on and on.

As soon as we arrived, Grandma introduced me around to all her co-workers. I was forced to endure a few hugs and a couple of kisses on the cheek. But after that, I was left to myself. Of course, there was plenty to do. I could read, explore the aisles lined with books, or write letters to my dad and Elizabeth and, if I ever forgave her, my mom. I found a table in a sunlit corner, tucked out of the way, and made myself comfortable.

"You come get me if you need anything," Grandma said.

"All right."

"I'm just down the aisle, right at the water fountain, through the double doors."

"Okay, got it."

"Anybody bothers you, you come get me."

"Yes, Grandma."

"And if you get hungry, I have—"

"Snacks in your purse," I finished for her.

Over the next few hours, I occasionally caught glimpses of her peeking at me from around the corner. That must have been enough to satisfy her. After that, she left me alone.

For my first few weeks in Seattle, that was our routine: work Monday, Wednesday, and Friday and then right back home afterwards. Mrs. Richards showed up most afternoons, dragging Tommy along to play on the piano. She called it "therapy." In my mind, I called it showing off. In fact, he was so good it made me sick to my stomach, and I decided then and there to give up any thought of playing the piano again. Why bother? No matter how much I practiced, I would always be mocked by the memory of how he played. Throw in choir practice on Wednesday night and church on Sunday, and I'm surprised I found time to even write a letter. When Grandma was done with work, she didn't waste any time. In other words, no dillydallying or dawdling. She'd march straight uphill toward home like she was trying to conquer Mt. Rainier, ignoring my hints and suggestions that it might be fun to look around and see the sights.

By the third week, I'd had enough. My campaign to get Grandma to send me home wasn't going anywhere. I'd tried mean and I'd tried nice, and nothing seemed to make a difference. I was beginning to think I might be stuck in Seattle for the whole summer after all. The thought of walking back home again and doing the same old things made me want to scream. So instead of following her up the hill, I stopped in the middle of the sidewalk outside the library entrance and announced, "I want to go another way."

"Excuse me?" she said, glancing back over her shoulder and coming to a halt.

"I'm tired of going home," I said forcefully. "Let's pretend we're tourists and go exploring. I'd like to see where Jimi Hendrix used to live. He's from Seattle, you know."

"Jimi Hendrix?"

"Guitar player. He's famous," I said.

"He can't be that famous," Grandma remarked.

"What do you mean?" I sputtered.

"If he's so famous, why haven't I heard of him before?" I was ready for her to shake her head and insist we continue on home. But after a moment, she shrugged and said, "Why not?" She marched back in my direction and grabbed my hand without breaking stride.

"Where are we going?" I asked, trotting to keep up with her.

"A surprise," my grandma said. "We can look for your famous friends some other time."

As we walked along, the buildings became smaller; the smells, richer and spicier; and the faces passing by, decidedly more Asian.

"Oh, I can guess where we're going," I said knowingly, unable to contain myself any longer. "Back home, we've got a place just like this," I announced, "only our Chinatown is bigger."

Grandma rolled her eyes and chuckled.

I managed to catch myself before I laughed along with her. I didn't want her to think I was going to be all grateful and everything just because she'd decided to break her routine this one time.

Our first stop, a placed called Hong's, was so filled with strong scents it made me sneeze. While I kept my nose plugged, Grandma picked up some tea. And then we walked across the street to Mr. Tan's fish market.

Sitting in mounds of ice on counters outside on the

sidewalk were rows of fresh fish and mounds of clams and oysters.

"Fresh this morning!" Mr. Tan exclaimed, his eyes twinkling as he wiped his hands on an apron stained with blood and fish guts.

"He always says that," Grandma muttered under her breath.

"There's *fresh*, Mr. Tan," she said more loudly, "and there's *fresh*, and I will be the judge of it."

"Can't never fool Miz St. Clair," Mr. Tan belly laughed.

"You've been here before?"

"Once or twice," Grandma said.

Two days later, instead of heading home right after work, Grandma grabbed my hand and marched me in the opposite direction.

"Another surprise?" I asked.

"You'll see," she said. I could tell she was having fun in spite of herself.

Twenty minutes later, we strolled into the big market at the end of Pike Street, on the hill above the sparkling blue waters of Elliott Bay.

At first, we just wandered the crowded rows amid vendors selling just about anything you could want or imagine, from trinkets to sunglasses to clothes to food.

Next, Grandma's nose led us to a small bakery that faced the street. It had a gleaming glass counter that was open to the sidewalk, letting the wonderful aroma of baked goodies drift up and down the street.

Grandma was such a tightwad, I figured we'd just look, but she paid for a couple of small loaves of fresh white bread, still warm, and a plastic container of freshly ground peanut butter, soft and oozy.

We found a couple of chairs out in front on the sidewalk. Then she tore apart the bread with her hands, spreading peanut butter on the warm insides with a plastic knife she always carried in her purse.

I watched her, mouth watering, the heady smell of bread and peanuts almost driving me crazy.

"Try this," Grandma said as she handed me a chunk.

"Thas iz munderful," I sighed a moment later, mouth thick with peanut butter and bread.

Street musicians were playing music on the corner nearby, so we listened while we ate. There were three of them, all longhaired, and they looked and dressed so much alike it was hard to tell the boys from the girls.

"Hippies!" Grandma snorted with disdain.

"Pretty good," I volunteered.

"Rank amateurs," Grandma snorted, fixing me with a hard, knowing stare that left me more than a bit confused.

*Must be the type of music*, I decided. *Hard to object to anyone singing about peace and love.* She probably preferred church music to what the hippies were playing.

When we were done with our snack, Grandma led me around the other way, even though the trio was still playing and the most direct way home led past them.

All of this leads up to why I was surprised when Grandma jerked me to a stop on our way back home. This time, instead of hippies, there was an old black man blowing on a harmonica. He was standing all by himself in the middle of the sidewalk, forcing everyone who wanted to get by to go out into the street or squeeze up against the side of the building. His hat was upside down on the concrete in front of him. I noticed a few coins inside it, but no bills.

I was ready to keep on going, but Grandma didn't budge.

*Not much to look at*, I thought to myself, giving him a once-over. Probably didn't smell good, either. His bald head was shiny with sweat. His face was like old shoe leather, wrinkled and craggy. His shabby old suit coat, baggy pants, and dusty shoes didn't improve my impression.

But as I listened to him play, I began to forget all about how he looked or smelled. Before long, I was swaying with the pulse of the wailing sound coming out of that small instrument he held over his mouth, cupped by his hand. I couldn't help it. I noticed Grandma couldn't keep still, either, her skirt swirling back and forth like a willow in a faint summer breeze.

When the song ended in a plaintive wail, I let out my breath, dizzy from not breathing. "Wow!" I said hoarsely.

"Now *that* is music," Grandma said.

"What's it called?" I asked.

"Blues," Grandma said. "Our people created it."

"Our people?"

"What do they teach kids nowadays?" Grandma muttered. "Our ancestors. Colored folks. Black people like you and me. Remember this. The blues were refined in the fire of hatred and oppression. There's nothing like them. Nothing. Long after this is all gone . . . " She gestured at the buildings around us and then continued, "people will still be talking about and listening to the blues. Mark my words."

She was shaking when she finished, staring at me fiercely like some ancient prophet.

A black woman beside us said, "Amen, sister." Grandma's face softened. She gave an embarrassed smile, finally noticing that everyone had been listening to her. She reached into her purse and dropped a five-dollar bill in the harmonica player's hat.

"Always wonderful to hear you play that harmonica, Sonny Ray," she said. "Now, make sure you come on by for pie and coffee, like I asked you last time. I'm still waiting."

A sheepish grin came across the man's weathered, walnut-colored face. He looked up at my grandma, his eyes watery. "Yes'm, Ruby," he said. "I've been meanin' to, but my feet been hurtin' so and that climb up that hill to your place is a long one."

"I won't take any excuses, Sonny Ray Johnson. You soak them in hot water and Epsom salts, put on a fresh pair of socks, and then come on up. The exercise will do you almost as much good as my pie."

Sonny glanced in my direction, and his smile brightened. "And who's the little lady?"

"This is my granddaughter, Maya. She is spending the summer with me."

"Pleased to make your acquaintance, miss," he said formally, touching his forehead.

I kept glancing at my grandma as we moved off. After all of that little episode, it was hard not to. Maybe there was more to her than I imagined.

"What are you staring at?" my grandma asked, finally.

"Nothin'."

"Oh, it isn't nothing. Out with it."

"I was just wondering about that bum back there. That Sonny Whatchimabobber—?"

"*Mister* Johnson and I go way back," she scolded. "He and I are longtime friends. In fact, we come from the same part of the country."

"And where is that?"

"Oklahoma," my grandma said, shaking her head. "But that was long, long ago."

"But—"

"No buts about it," my grandma interrupted. "I remember my friends. That's all there is to it."

I had a dozen more questions to ask, but by then, I was huffing and puffing so much, trying to keep up with her as we began the long uphill climb to her house, that I couldn't say another word.

# Chapter Fifteen

A week or so after the Fourth of July, Grandma and I trooped up the porch steps, all hot and tired from our long climb uphill.

Even Grandma, who never seemed to get out of breath, was open-mouthed by the time we reached her porch, dabbing at the moisture on her forehead with a fresh white handkerchief.

I was thinking about visiting the Garcias down the street, to see if they might like to play some baseball. When the Garcias had visitors, we often had enough kids for two teams. I didn't even mind when Grandma made me bring Tommy along. Of course, he never played. I'm not even sure he was aware of what we were doing. But he made a pretty good second base. For a human, that is. I'd stand him in place, give him something to examine, and he would stay put like a statue for most of the game.

As soon as Grandma unlocked the front door, I

pushed past her, scrambling to pick up the mail scattered across the hardwood floor, feeling the sour wash of disappointment when there was nothing from my dad. *Tomorrow*, I vowed to myself, aware of Grandma watching me, her mouth a thin line.

I handed her the stack and began calling Harry S. He was usually lounging on the cool floor, acting like he wasn't waiting for us.

But this time he wasn't there.

"Harry S.?" I yelled. "Here kitty, kitty, kitty."

Grandma closed the door, hung her purse on the coat rack, and then began to sort through the mail.

"Just junk mail," I remarked.

"Oh, for goodness' sake," she snapped with exasperation. "Why don't you let me decide what is junk and what is not?"

"Suit yourself," I muttered quietly. And then I called more loudly: "Harry S. !"

"He's probably taking it easy in an open window somewhere," Grandma remarked. "Hot day like this, that is where we should have been, instead of hiking up Mt. Rainier."

I trotted into the front room, to the big windowsill next to the grand piano. It was one of Harry S.'s favorite places.

No Harry S.

I called again, starting to get mad and worried at the same time. "Now cut that out, Harry S. Here kitty, kitty, kitty."

I dogtrotted into the kitchen. Still no Harry.

I was on my way back out to the front hallway when there was a knock on the front door.

Grandma had already kicked off one shoe. "Now what?" she remarked. She fixed her hair and then turned the knob.

The door was barely halfway open when Mrs. Richards pushed it in the rest of the way and rushed past my grandma. "Have you seen Tommy?" she burst out. She didn't sound all that panicked, but the way she was wringing her hands immediately got my attention.

"What's wrong?" Grandma asked.

"Tommy—I can't find him. I've looked everywhere. I turned away for just a minute or two, and, and—"

"How long has he been gone?"

Mrs. Richards pushed her hair back off her forehead and considered. "Ten minutes or so. It seems so much longer."

I nodded as I listened to her. Time has a freaky way of being kind of hard to keep track of, I knew, from firsthand experience. Lately, I'd begun sneaking out of the library, exploring the blocks surrounding the big old building. I'd even found a place that had free sodas and music. It was called Students for a Free America. It reminded me of the places I used to visit with my mom—before we'd started arguing and fighting, that is.

Even though I was younger than everyone else there, they let me hang around. It was probably because I helped make posters and didn't act stupid.

In fact, I'd been working on a poster just that morning, painting *GET US OUT NOW* in big red letters, making the O's in *OUT* and *NOW* into peace signs. Of course, it was all about getting us out of that war in Vietnam, something I was happy to support, since that would bring my dad home all the sooner.

While I worked, I'd been listening to a longhaired, pimple-faced college boy who didn't look much older than me, who was trying to impress a girl nearby. He was going on and on about Einstein, and I could tell he was boring the girl half to death. It was pathetic.

Of course, I didn't understand much of what he said, but I had been intrigued when he commented that of course everyone knew that time wasn't constant. It could go faster or slower, depending on certain things, like whether you were traveling at the speed of light or not.

I knew that Mr. Einstein had it right. After all, I'd ex-

perienced it myself on my bus ride north a few weeks earlier, though we'd only been going sixty miles per hour, not
screaming along at 186,000 miles per second.

And now Mrs. Richards had experienced it, too.

"You, you haven't seen him, have you?" she asked,
her voice rising sharply. "He isn't in here?" She rushed
into the front room, where my grandma kept the grand piano.

"No," Grandma replied. "We've just arrived home and
have not seen him. If he came by earlier, we were not
here."

"Oh, dear," Mrs. Richards moaned, her proper English facade melting like a dish of ice cream that had sat too
long in the heat.

"Maya?" Grandma said sharply.

"Yes."

"Take Mrs. Richards into the living room and have
her sit down for a moment. I'm going to call the police."

I led Mrs. Richards to a chair. Grandma was right behind us a moment later with what looked like a glass of
water. She handed it to Mrs. Richards, who took a quick
sip and then stared up at my grandma, her eyes widening.

"Does this have . . . ?"

"A little extra something," my grandma finished for
her, glancing in my direction. "Something for your
nerves," she added, apologetically.

128

Mrs. Richards finished the rest in one gulp.

"The police are on the way," Grandma said. "I explained what happened, and I told them about Tommy's condition. I hope you don't mind."

"No, that's quite all right," Mrs. Richards said, her voice shaking.

"Maya will stay here and wait for them. You and I will start looking. He can't have gone far."

"Yes, yes, indeed," Mrs. Richards said. "Of course, I should be out looking for him."

"What about Harry S.?" I blurted out. Tommy could take care of himself, but Harry S. was just a poor, defenseless cat and I was worried about him.

Grandma looked at me, her eyes dark and serious, and I knew it was time to quit squawking about the cat.

"Why don't I look for Tommy in the backyard?" I suggested.

"No," Grandma said sharply. "You wait here, right by the door, just like I said. When the police show up, you tell them again what happened and what Mrs. Richards and I are doing. And *then* you go look in the backyard. For Tommy and not that cat. Got it?"

I nodded. Sometimes it's better not arguing with an adult.

Grandma and Mrs. Richards flew out the door as if

pushed along by a cyclone. When they were safely on the sidewalk, I wandered out onto the porch to wait for the police.

They talked strategy for a moment, then Grandma headed one way and Mrs. Richards the other, their voices filling the heavy afternoon air: "Tommy! Tommy!"

Grandma paused at Mrs. Garcia's house down the street. I couldn't see the other side of the conversation, but I could imagine Mrs. Garcia leaning out her kitchen window, asking what all the hullabaloo was about.

A few moments later, Mrs. Garcia joined in the search, still wearing her pink slippers.

My grandma pointed across the street, like a general directing troops. Mrs. Garcia nodded and hurried off in that direction.

*Nothing for me to do but sit here and wait*, I thought grumpily. Worst of all, I seemed to be the only one who cared that Harry S. might be in mortal danger.

# Chapter Sixteen

Moments later, after Grandma, Mrs. Garcia, and Mrs. Richards had disappeared from view, a police car skidded to a stop in front of the house, its lights flashing. I waited for the officer to open the door before hopping off the front porch to meet him.

"Your mother around?" the officer drawled, looking at me from behind dark sunglasses.

"Nossir," I replied.

"Any grown-ups around?" he said, trying again.

"Nossir."

That caused a faint smile and a shake of the head. "Hot day, ain't it?" he said, adjusting the big, black belt that held in his belly and then leaning back on the front fender of the police car.

"Yessir."

"Why don't you tell me what's going on, then?" he said, pulling a notebook out of his shirt pocket. "Something about a missing child?"

"Yessir. His name is Tommy. He lives over there." I pointed to the house next door. "He took off a while ago. His mom can't find him, so now she and my grandmother and Mrs. Garcia are looking for him."

"I see," said the police officer. "Got a description?"

"He's a boy. And, uh, about this tall." I held up my arm. "Brownish hair and—"

"He colored?" the police officer interrupted.

"Nossir," I replied peevishly, wondering what that had to do with anything, "and if you keep interrupting me, I'm going to get all messed up." I put my hands on my hips.

He dipped his head, touching the bill of his cap. "Sorry, ma'am," he said.

"As I was about to say, I figure he's the whitest boy I've ever seen. You got that?"

"Yes, ma'am. Do you happen to know what he's wearing?"

"I don't know," I said truthfully. I hadn't seen Tommy that morning. Even if I had, he usually messed up a shirt or two during the day, so he always seemed to be in different clothes.

"Uh-huh," nodded the officer. "You say the mom and some others are off looking for him?"

I nodded. By the sound of their voices, they were already a block away. The police officer heard the hollering right about then, too.

"The mother?" he asked, eyebrows peeking out over the top of his sunglasses.

"She went thataway," I said. "She's wearing a light blue dress."

The police officer yawned, fixed his sunglasses on me again, and then wandered back to his car.

*Must be fun*, I thought, as the car roared off down the street, *hot-rodding around the city in a nice car, blasting the siren whenever you want everyone to get out of your way.*

Maybe that's what I'd be when I was old enough. Forget college. It was easy to imagine how cool I'd look in a uniform, that big black belt, and sunglasses.

I was still thinking about it when I remembered what Grandma had said about searching the backyard for Tommy.

Halfway up the steps, it occurred to me that it wouldn't hurt if I delayed carrying out her orders for a little while. It wasn't really being disobedient. Not exactly.

Instead of going straight to the backyard, I headed for the kitchen and made myself a peanut butter and honey sandwich. I didn't think a slight detour would hurt. And because it was so hot, I decided to treat myself to a can of ice-cold soda pop. Grape, of course.

And then, because I was still hungry after eating the sandwich, I helped myself to a handful of cookies. I ate two and stuck the rest of them in my pocket. Only then was I ready to begin the search for Tommy. I let the screen door close with a gunshot bang.

As I stood on the back porch, devouring another cookie, I scanned the backyard. There were only a few places Tommy could be hiding. I trotted over to the big bush Grandma called a rhododendron and checked behind it, then I moved on, using a stick to poke into a wild tangle of bushes in need of a haircut.

I figured if Tommy was back there, he'd see that stick coming at him and move out of the way. Worst case, he'd get jabbed a little bit—a small price to pay for taking off like that.

Unfortunately, when I was done looking, there was still no Tommy and no Harry S. Just some old newspaper, all wet and nasty-looking, and a couple of baseballs, green with mold, leftovers from some long-ago game.

The baseballs were an unexpected find. If I cleaned them up, I could use them when I played baseball with the Garcias or drive Grandma and Mrs. Richards crazy by bouncing them off the garage door.

My obligations satisfied, I opened the can of pop and headed back to the house. It was time to resume my search for one missing Missouri cat named Harry S. Truman. He was probably sleeping somewhere inside, too hot to get up and let us know he was alive.

For some strange reason, as I climbed up the back steps, my eyes wandered up the side of the house. I'm not sure why. Maybe I heard a plane flying by overhead. Or caught some slight movement out of the corner of my eye. Or maybe it was an angel lifting my chin.

In any case, I looked up, and there, framed behind a small dusty window near the peak of the roof, was Harry S. Truman himself. What brought me to a dead stop was who was holding him.

Yeah, it was Tommy.

I was so stunned I just stood there, open-mouthed, for what seemed like forever. That darned Einstein again.

The spell crumbled when I noticed Tommy's hands. They weren't stroking Harry S.'s fur, friendly and nice. Instead they were around his neck, squeezing.

If that wasn't bad enough, what stabbed me right in the heart was the look on Harry S.'s face. He seemed to be saying, "Are you just going to stand there, or are you going to come up here and save me?"

# Chapter Seventeen

I gave an angry bellow, flung open the back door, pounded through the kitchen and around the corner, and dashed upstairs, taking two steps at a time. I raced past my bedroom, the bathroom door, and my grandma's bedroom, then came to a skidding halt in front of that door at the end of the hallway.

I turned the doorknob. The door opened with a faint creak.

Of course, I'd tried that door on numerous occasions over the past few weeks. Even the tricks I'd learned from Elizabeth's brother hadn't worked on it. For just a brief moment, I wondered how Tommy had managed to get it open. That sneak. But now wasn't the time to consider how he'd done it.

I took a deep breath and then stomped up those dusty stairs, screaming, yelling, and threatening Tommy (and any spiders that happened to be listening) with serious bodily harm if they bent so much as a hair on poor Harry S. Truman's head.

The window where Tommy had been standing was off to my left and easy enough to find.

There was only one problem. Tommy and Harry S. were gone.

A pale shaft of sunlight sliced across the room, which was choked with furniture covered in sheets and old blankets, stacks of boxes of nearly every shape and size, tables, trunks, wardrobes, and racks heavy with old clothes. Everything was coated with a thin layer of dust. It looked like a baker had gone mad long ago, flinging flour everywhere.

And then I heard a sound.

It came from far in the corner.

I was off, dodging between stacks of boxes like a running back. When old clothes on a line blocked my way, I simply ducked my head and plowed right through.

I came out on the other side, sneezing from all the dust, and that's when I saw them. Tommy had his knees pulled up to his chest, head down. One arm was draped over Harry S. Truman, who was lying stretched out on the floor next to him, eyes closed.

"You killed him!" I screamed, clenching my hands into rock-hard fists. I took a step forward.

Harry S. Truman opened his eyes. He looked up at me like there was nothing out of the ordinary going on, yawned, and then meowed hello.

I hesitated, blinking a couple of times, just to make sure I wasn't imagining it all. Harry S. wasn't dead? But he had to be dead. I had seen Tommy's hands clenched around his neck. And yet here he was, flopped down next to Tommy like they were the best of friends.

Harry S. licked a paw and then began to scrub his face, worrying about his looks at a time like this.

I felt so dizzy and sick to my stomach from all the excitement that I dropped my fists and sat down next to them, all my anger deflated.

I don't remember how long we sat there. But after a while, when I started feeling better, I remembered the cookies in my pocket. They were mostly crumbs by now, but I fished out the bigger pieces, stuck a couple in my mouth, and started sucking the sugar out of them.

I heard Tommy sniff. He was still huddled in the corner; he hadn't moved. He seemed to be peering at me from between the fingers covering his eyes, watching me suck on those bits of cookie.

"You want some cookie?"

I held out my hand, and then I remembered a comment Mrs. Richards had made about Tommy not liking

people to look straight at him. I had read that some animals were the same way. Bullies, too. They took a direct
look as a challenge. Harry S., on the other hand, didn't
seem to care one way or the other. Sometimes, he'd look
right back at me, and other times, he'd look away, as if he
didn't want to be bothered.

I decided to see what Tommy would do if I didn't pay
him any attention. I let my eyes wander around the attic,
but I didn't bother to hide my smile when I felt him take a
couple of pieces of cookie from my hand.

When I glanced at him, his fingers were already back
over his face, but I could see his chin moving as he
chewed.

Harry S. stood, arched his back, and yawned, announcing it was time to go. He was right. I'd waited long
enough. If I didn't let Grandma know that I'd found
Tommy soon, she and Mrs. Richards would mobilize the
entire city.

As I started to get up, Tommy stopped me. "Play," he
said. I admit I was surprised. Except for those screeches
and screams that first time—and they didn't really count—
I had never heard him speak before. He had a nice enough
voice, soft and sweet like that of a boy who was much
younger.

"No, we can't play right now," I replied, some of my

peevishness creeping back into my voice. "I gotta let everyone know you're okay."

"Play," he said again, louder. He patted the case lying on the floor beside him and began rocking back and forth.

I eyed him for a moment, and then I realized what he wanted. "You want me to look inside that?" I said.

Tommy seemed to rock even harder.

"Okay," I said, more to myself than to him. "But then I gotta let people know that you're okay before we both get in trouble."

I slid next to him and looked the case over. It was bigger than a briefcase and too oddly shaped for a suitcase, long and narrow instead of square. Despite the layer of dust, the color came through easily enough. Brown. The outside was cracked and battered, covered with faded stickers from faraway places like Miami Beach . . . Scranton . . . and Paris.

The latches were already undone. I glared at Tommy. He had been snooping.

I flipped open the lid and stared down at what was inside.

"Play," Tommy cried again.

There, gleaming bright gold against the dark blue velvet, was some sort of musical instrument. It was all in pieces, so I couldn't tell what it was. It didn't look like a trumpet. Too long and too big. It didn't look like a tuba either; it was much too small. Whatever it was, I had to admit it was one of the most beautiful things I had ever seen.

"You found this?"

Tommy stopped rocking for just a moment, then resumed. I took that as his way of saying yes.

As I reached out to caress the bell, I heard a faraway slam and the sound of my name drifting up the stairs.

I reluctantly flipped the lid closed. This would have to wait. "Come on, you," I said. I grabbed Tommy by the hand and began to pull him along behind me.

At first, he held back like an ornery mule, but I'd already been nice enough. I yanked his arm hard, not caring if I hurt him, and he fell into line.

"We're coming," I yelled.

# Chapter Eighteen

That night, as I lay in bed, going over the events of the day, I still felt like a hero.

When we had appeared at the top of the stairs, Mrs. Richards had reacted the way any mother would, American, English, or African. She'd taken the steps two at a time, hugged her son tight, and then begun crying with relief.

Mrs. Garcia, crowded in the doorway with two of her older boys, hadn't been able to stop saying "Gracias a Dios!" Towering behind her, even the police officer had managed a smile. When he spotted me, he'd pulled his sunglasses down on the end of his nose and winked.

As I stepped off the bottom stair, even Grandma had grabbed me, squeezing me so tight that it left me gasping for air.

"Did you find him in the backyard?" she asked, pushing me out to arm's length, searching my face with those worn eyes.

"No, ma'am," I said. "I looked and poked around, but I didn't see anything. I was going back in the house when I noticed Harry S. and Tommy up in the attic window." I kept quiet about the fact that it had looked like Tommy was right in the middle of committing cat murder.

"The attic?" Grandma exclaimed.

I nodded. "Tommy must have slipped out of his house, just like everybody thought. But instead of taking off for the streets, he wandered over here, probably wanting to play the piano."

"You some sort of female Sherlock Holmes or something?" said the officer from the doorway where he was standing.

I ignored his comment. "When he found the front door locked," I continued, "he must have gone around to the back and used that door to get in the house."

"But the attic?" Grandma said again. "How did he find his way up there? He's never even been upstairs before. I don't even think he's been out of the living room. And that door is always locked. How did he get in?"

I paused and glared at the culprit, Harry S. "I bet Tommy followed the cat upstairs. No telling what attracted them to the door at the end of the hallway. But he must have beelined toward it. Maybe piano isn't his only talent.

Once he got the door open, he climbed up to the attic, accompanied by his partner in crime, a sneaky feline named Harry S. Truman."

"My word," Mrs. Richards said.

"There was plenty up in the attic to keep a cat and a kid busy. I doubt they heard all the commotion downstairs. It was just lucky timing that Tommy and Harry S. happened to be standing in front of the window at the very moment I looked up."

That's when Harry S. Truman decided to join the celebration. He came sashaying down the stairs like the most innocent creature in Eden.

"But of course," Grandma said, looking down at him as he brushed by her leg. She covered a smile with her hand. "I should have known Tommy couldn't get into this much trouble all by himself."

"It wasn't the cat's fault," Mrs. Richards said, looking sheepish. "Maya's right. Piano isn't Tommy's only talent. He's been known to get himself into the unlikeliest places. The day before we left England, we found him curled up in the boot of the Rover."

"Boot?" Grandma said.

"Rover?" I added.

Mrs. Richards looked blankly at us for a moment, then giggled. "Oh, dear. I see how that must sound. A

Rover is an automobile, not a dog. And let me see, you folks would say *hatch*. No, that's not right, either.

"You mean *trunk*," the officer said.

"Quite right," Mrs. Richards agreed. "Thank you."

"No problem," the officer said. "Nice to be of some help."

"I suppose I'll need to lock the back door from now on," Grandma mused to herself.

"It wouldn't help," Mrs. Richards said. "A locked door has never stopped him before. On the other hand . . . " she paused, and I could see the panic growing in her eyes as she considered all the possibilities. "I'd be jolly well pleased if you *didn't* lock that door. What if Tommy had found the back door locked as well and instead of breaking in, he decided not to bother. . . . There's no telling where in bloody hell he could've ended up. . . . " At this point, she began to cry again.

That was the signal for everyone to begin clearing out. The police officer touched the tip of his cap and strolled back to his car. Mrs. Garcia waved good-bye and then herded her children back home. Mrs. Richards mouthed a thank-you in my direction and then, clutching Tommy close to her as if she was afraid he might skedaddle off somewhere else, went home.

"You did a good thing today, Maya," said Grandma,

interrupting my reverie. She was standing in the doorway, outlined by the light from the hall.

"It was nothing," I said, wondering again if I should tell her what I thought Tommy had been doing to Harry S. Instead, I decided to ask her about something safe. "Guess what Tommy found up there?"

"I have no idea," she said.

"He found some sort of musical instrument in a funny old case . . . and that seemed to set him off. He kept saying, 'play,' like he thought it was some sort of toy. I had no idea he could even talk, though I always figured him for sneaky. . . . Anyway, it was covered with stickers—the case, I mean. I opened it up, and there it was, all gold and shiny—"

"Billy Bones's trombone," my grandma breathed, interrupting the tumble of words.

"Billy Bones?" I sat up. There was that name again.

"I had forgotten it was up there," she said, so softly I could tell she was just talking mostly to herself. "I'm sorry, Maya."

"Sorry for what?" I was becoming more confused by the second.

Because of the light shining from the hallway behind her, Grandma's face was a mask of shadows. It was hard to tell if she was really sorry or just saying the words, the way most people do.

"Billy Bones," she sighed. "That was his nickname, his performing name. His real name was William Reginald St. Clair. That was his trombone you found. Do you know he won it in a footrace? Wasn't much older than you. First prize. There was some cash or that old trombone, and a lot of grumbling because he was a black boy and he'd outrun a passel of white boys. He picked the trombone instead of the money. Safer, he figured. I'm not sure it was true, but I don't think he ever regretted it."

"But who the heck was he?" I asked, exasperated.

Grandma blinked. "Why, he was your grandfather!"

That took a moment to sink in. To be honest, I had never really given my grandpa much thought.

"You don't know anything about him, do you?"

I shrugged. Grandpa, Billy Bones, even William— they were all just names for some stranger. I wanted to feel something. But I didn't. They were just names, nothing more.

Grandma turned her face sideways. I could see it in the light, then, see how she closed her eyes tight, her face suddenly looking old and pained. "Your mom never knew much about him, either," she said. "He died before she was born. I didn't talk about him much. I was too busy trying to make a living. I guess it was just too painful. I never did forgive him, you know, for going off like that and getting himself killed, leaving me all alone and pregnant with your mom. Maybe you know something about people you love going off and leaving—"

I opened my mouth, ready to yell "SHUT UP," but she didn't stop there, and then the moment was gone.

"But all that doesn't seem to matter much anymore," she said. "So this is who Billy Bones was. . . . He was your grandfather, your mom's daddy, my husband, and he was a wonderful man. He was also a musician. One of the best these parts has ever seen. And he played just about the best kind of music there is—blues and jazz. Oh my, could he play."

"Sounds like you loved him very much," I offered cautiously, not quite sure what to make of this new, vulnerable grandma. "I'm sorry he's dead," I added, not because I was actually sorry, but because, well, sometimes it's better to say something than nothing at all.

"Me too," she said. I heard her take a deep breath. She shook her head as if to rid herself of the memories, good and bad. "Long past your bedtime."

"I'd like to hear more about him sometime. . . . You know, Billy Bones," I said, wondering, for the first time since I had arrived, if maybe my grandma wasn't a dried-up old prune after all.

"Yes, sometime," she repeated, her voice cracking

with fatigue and something else I knew all too well. "But not tonight." I heard the floor creak as she shifted her weight and then disappeared down the hall.

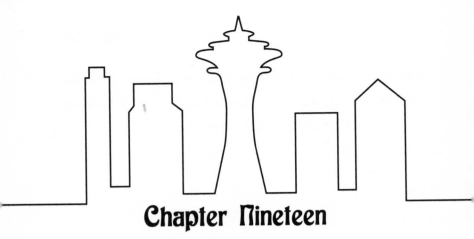

# Chapter Nineteen

The next afternoon, there was a knock at the door. I came skidding around the corner in my socks, just as Tommy marched in as if he owned the place.

But instead of heading for the piano as I expected, he stomped right past me and on up the stairs.

"Hey!" I yelled. "The piano's thataway."

But Tommy didn't skip a beat. He kept on going as if he didn't hear me at all. I can't say I was surprised. That was, well, Tommy.

Just as he disappeared from view at the top of the stairs, Mrs. Richards pulled open the screen door and stepped into the house, making sure to wipe her sandals first.

As usual, she was wearing a long, flowing skirt and a sleeveless top that highlighted her pale skin.

The skirt was what caught my eye. I'd never been a fan of dresses or skirts. But that afternoon, I couldn't take my eyes off her skirt. It was splashed with bright patches of purple that seemed to glow in the afternoon sunshine.

"Ah, Petula," Grandma said, drying her hands on her apron and stepping out of the kitchen. "A little less excitement today."

"Good afternoon, Ruby," Mrs. Richards replied, craning her neck to see into the living room and noticing right away that Tommy wasn't sitting at the piano.

"He's gone upstairs," I chirped, pointing with a finger. "Probably heading for all those poisons and pills in the medicine cabinet," I added.

Mrs. Richards blew out her cheeks with exasperation, but before she could do anything about it, Grandma jumped in. "Oh, shush, Maya," she said. "You know as well as I do that he's probably gone back to the attic with that cat. I'll send you after him in a few minutes," she said, pointing at me.

"I suppose it's all right," Mrs. Richards said, that worried, haunted look around her mouth relaxing. "At least we know where he is."

"You're welcome to sit for a spell," Grandma said, "or follow me into the kitchen and we can chat. I'm making bread today."

But Mrs. Richards was already rummaging through her bag. "I brought a little something—a thank-you—for all your help yesterday," she said, handing me an oddly shaped candy bar. "Oh, it's English," she said, seeing the look on my face and smiling. "English chocolate. I think you'll like it."

"Cool," I said.

"Maya," my grandmother growled softly.

"Way cool. . . . I mean, thank you so very much," I added quickly.

"And some English tea for you, Ruby. I'm sorry it isn't more, but—"

"No apologies," Grandma interrupted briskly. "We were more than glad to help out. I'll boil some water. Join me for a cup?"

As they headed for the kitchen, I sat down on the bottom stair and tried out that English chocolate.

After the first bite, I knew Mrs. Richards was right. *Spoiled forever*, I thought as I took another bite, half listening to the chatter of the two women in the kitchen and wondering what Tommy was up to now.

I decided to wait until I was done with the chocolate before finding out.

He beat me to it.

Halfway through the candy bar, I heard a noise at the top of the stairs. I turned around, and there he was, wearing an old suit jacket that hung down past his knees, a hat that looked like it had once done duty as a fruit bowl, and a pair of battered shoes, turned up at the toes.

But what interested me even more than his exotic outfit was the case he was dragging behind him. It bounced harshly on every step as he came clumping downstairs.

I gulped down the last bite of chocolate and got out of his way.

Of course, Grandma and Mrs. Richards had heard the noise. They joined me, watching as Tommy stepped off the last stair and stopped. He laid the case down on the wood floor right at my feet, flipped the latches, opened the top, pointed at the pieces of Billy Bones's trombone inside it, and shouted, "PLAY!"

# Chapter Twenty

"My goodness," Grandma exclaimed. "What's gotten into him?"

"I don't know," Mrs. Richards said, giving me a strange look as Harry S. Truman streaked down the stairs, leapt over the case, and then sauntered into the fray. He rubbed against Tommy's leg and looked up at me in a way that said it all.

"Traitor," I hissed, glaring back at him.

As usual, Tommy wasn't paying any attention to Harry S. It was hard to tell what was going through his mind. I could only guess. But something was egging him on. Then, strange as ever, without another word or sound, he stood up, turned on his heel, and left.

I watched him angle into the living room. He sat down at the piano, flipped back his coattails like a concert pianist, pushed up his sleeves, and immediately began playing a song with a distinctive beat—da doo daaah doo da-daaah doo da.

"What's that?" I asked no one in particular.

"'Satin Doll,'" Grandma and Mrs. Richards said in unison.

"Tommy heard it for the first time on the radio last night," Mrs. Richards added, shaking her head in wonder.

"And he's already playing it like a young Duke Ellington," Grandma exclaimed. "Imagine that."

"I'm still not used to it," Mrs. Richards remarked. "They still can't explain it at the university."

Her statement made my grandmother break out in laughter. "What's to explain? Take it as a gift from the Almighty. Just like him, too. You figure he isn't paying attention to any of us down here, and then he goes and surprises you."

"I suppose that's one way to look at it," Mrs. Richards said dryly. "Seems like a mean-spirited trick to me."

I squatted down next to the trombone, deciding it was time to take a closer look.

"Play," Tommy had said, just like yesterday in the attic. It seemed clear—at least to me—that he was talking directly to me. And it seemed clear what he wanted me to do: play this trombone.

I had to admit that I was attracted to the instrument. When I looked at it, I felt a kind of faint electricity buzzing softly in the background and I had a strange sense that I was following a script somebody else had written.

Somehow, Tommy was meant to find my grandfather's trombone and I was meant to try and play it. Maybe this was that elusive something I had been looking for—and didn't find—when I explored the house soon after I had first arrived.

I checked to make sure I'd licked all the chocolate off my fingers, and then I touched the dark blue velvet that covered the inside of the case. It was more worn than I had noticed earlier, but it was still as soft as the fur on Harry S.'s white belly.

The trombone looked like it was made of solid gold, bright despite a thin layer of dust. Looking closely, I noticed there was a faint, intricate pattern swirling over the bell, etched like fine embroidery. That trombone may not have been worth a million bucks, but as far as I was concerned, it was priceless.

I ran the back of my hand along its surface. It was smooth and cold and made me shiver a little.

"It's a beautiful trombone," Mrs. Richards remarked. "Whose is it?"

"My grandfather's," I said.

"What kind of music did he play?" Mrs. Richards asked.

"Jazz and blues," Grandma answered. "Of course, he could play just about anything," she added, her voice getting stronger as she warmed to the subject. "Ragtime. Dixieland. Even orchestra music. I heard him play the Bach Cello Suites once. It was, well, it was one of the most beautiful things I've ever heard."

In the next room, Tommy finished a run up the keyboard and then bellowed, "PLAY!"

The three of us stared at each other for a moment, and then we all burst out laughing.

"Sorry," Mrs. Richards said, with an embarrassed wave of her hand. "He doesn't understand that trombones aren't, well, suitable musical instruments for girls."

"Says who?" I said, my eyes narrowing.

"Well, it's just understood, isn't it? Violin or cello, flute—there are any number of instruments more suitable to female sensibilities."

"Female what?" I could not believe what I was hearing. From the frown on Grandma's face, neither could she.

I pulled the largest piece, the bell, out of the case and started blowing in the small end. It made a loud, harsh noise that sounded like a squawking goose.

Before Mrs. Richards could say "I told you so," Grandma grabbed the bell from my hands. "For goodness' sake," she exclaimed. "Give me that before someone thinks I'm dying in here and calls the police."

She settled onto the floor next to the case. "Let me

show you how it works. First, you put these two pieces together."

She took the bell from my hand and then pulled the other pieces from their slots in the case. "This is the slide," she said, her voice slipping into a cadence I hadn't heard before. She slid the two pieces together and then tightened the locking nut.

"You put the mouthpiece in here," she said, opening a little pocket and pulling out the mouthpiece, then twisting it into the open end of the slide. "It's where you blow like the dickens, buzzing your lips to make a sound."

She took a deep breath, pursed her lips as if she was going to kiss a frog, and then blew into the mouthpiece. A rich, clear tone filled the room, startling all of us.

"Play!" Tommy yelled triumphantly, clapping his hands twice and then turning his attention back to the piano.

"I couldn't do that again even if I wanted to," Grandma chuckled. "You move the slide back and forth and make your lips tighter or looser when you want to change notes. Billy had a word for it, but I don't remember what it's called."

"Embouchure," Mrs. Richards said, with a blush. "It's called changing your embouchure."

Grandma and I just stared at her.

She began playing with her hair, glancing at the ceiling. "Oh, all right," she said in a rush of confession. "I used to play my brother's trumpet when he wasn't around. Fancied myself becoming a musician until my mother put a stop to it."

"I'm sorry," I blurted out. I wondered if that was where she got the idea that girls shouldn't play this kind of instrument.

"Me, too," Mrs. Richards squeaked.

Grandma decided to bring the conversation back to the instrument at hand. She cleared her throat and said, "It's pretty simple, actually. Not much more than some brass tubing, twisted into different shapes and dimensions."

She demonstrated again. The note rang out, dipping down as she moved the slide out and rising when she pulled it back.

"Can I try?" I asked, my voice trembling with growing excitement.

Grandma propped the trombone on my left shoulder. I blew into the mouthpiece, tentatively at first, making it buzz like a fly at the window.

"Don't be shy," she said. "You can't hurt it. Buzz your lips and blow like you want to pop a window out of its frame."

I closed my eyes, took a deep breath, and then blew

from the bottom of my toes. Magically, a note as clear as the one my grandmother had played filled the room.

"Here, you can do it by yourself," Grandma said, smiling, letting me hold the instrument without her help. "You're just like your grandfather."

She listened to me play a few more notes, then turned to Mrs. Richards. "Help me up, please. How about some more tea? You might like to hear about one of my friends. A mighty fine jazz trombonist—some thought better than even my Billy—though I might argue with them."

"Certainly," Mrs. Richards replied. "That would be quite lovely."

"Her name is Melba," Grandma said, winking in my direction.

"Can I keep playing?" I said, with a giggle.

"That old horn isn't going to mind," Grandma said, "and I don't suppose Billy would, either."

# Chapter Twenty-One

Most of the time, I would play the trombone upstairs in the attic. It was quiet and out of the way. I sat on a chair near the window, experimenting with different sounds, moving the slide in and out and blowing, imagining how Grandpa must have sounded.

There was no heat in the attic, so on chilly, rainy days, I pulled on whatever I could find up there to stay warm.

In one old suitcase, I came across a shiny black jacket that still smelled faintly of tobacco and aftershave. Of course, it was too big, but that made it just about perfect. It was long enough to cover my bare legs and would keep me warm, just like a blanket. All I had to do was roll up the sleeves.

In an old box, I found a stack of hats like the ones I'd discovered downstairs. I picked through them until I came across a beautiful gray fedora with a black satin band. I perched it on the back of my head. It was perfect.

It must have been a strange sight: a thirteen-year-old black girl, sitting on a battered chair in a pool of rain-filtered light, squawking on an old trombone and wearing a dead man's jacket and hat.

Whenever Tommy came over to play the piano, I lugged the trombone downstairs, leaving behind the jacket and hat. I did my best to try to play along with him, but it was frustrating because Tommy was a genius. He sounded like he had been playing the piano for years, while the honks I made sounded like an old moose.

But he didn't seem to care.

From the way his feet bobbed and his legs swung back and forth when I was trying to play along, he even seemed to like it.

But I cared how I sounded. I wasn't content with being just a beginner. After all, I'd been taking piano lessons for years with Mrs. Friermuth. I wanted to learn some real songs, not just make a lot of noise. That's when I decided to ask my grandma about trombone lessons. I figured, *what's the worst she could say—no?*

"Why?" she asked, not bothering to look up from her crocheting. She was sitting in a rocking chair in the backyard. Just "enjoyin' God's fresh air," as she described it.

I thought for a moment before I answered. "Because I stink."

That got her attention. "Excuse me?"

"I mean, I don't sound very good. I'd like to get a few pointers, some starter lessons. I already know how to read music, so that's gotta count for something."

I could see Grandma giving me the eye, wondering, I suppose, if this had anything to do with lessons or was simply cover for some other sinister scheme.

"Lessons take time and cost money. You certainly have the time, but what about the money?"

I thought of the $38.53 I had hidden away and then shrugged.

"So, you're thinking somebody is going to give you lessons out of the goodness of their heart?"

I shrugged again.

"Oh, I see. You think your nice ol' grandma would be willing to pay for the lessons?"

I gave her a wide-eyed look. "I thought you could talk to my mom—"

"She's got better things to do with her money," Grandma said with a snort, returning to her crochet.

"Maybe we could work out a trade or something?" I suggested.

"We'll see," Grandma said, not even bothering to think about it.

"What does that mean?" I said, a little sass creeping into my voice. But if Grandma heard it, she didn't respond.

"It means what it means," she said, signaling with the tone of her voice that the subject was closed for the time being.

Of course, if she thought that was going to stop my trombone playing, I was more than happy to disappoint her. I kept playing upstairs in the attic and downstairs with Tommy.

In fact, I don't think I could have stopped if I had wanted to.

Of course, I didn't play the trombone all the time. When I wasn't playing or helping Grandma with chores, I sometimes helped Mrs. Richards with Tommy's exercises. That's what she called them. To me, they were just games—the kind of games you'd play with a baby, not with a kid as old as Tommy. Sometimes, we'd just push a ball back and forth across the floor. Other times, I'd show him pictures and then say the words: *dog, cat, mouse, orange, chocolate.*

Sometimes, Harry S. would sit next to Tommy, staring intently at the cards as I showed them one by one. I suppose that's when I realized how much alike they were. I had noticed Harry staring intensely at dust particles sparkling in a band of sunlight, and then I'd noticed Tommy doing the same thing. I even wondered if Tommy was more like a cat than a human being.

Still, it didn't surprise me when Tommy learned to say "chocolate." It probably helped that I'd sneak him M&Ms when I'd say the word. Mrs. Richards was ecstatic the first time she heard him say it.

"We're working on *Mummy*," I assured her. But she didn't seem to care.

I suppose it was odd that a couple of kids preferred to spend perfect summer days indoors, playing games and music, rather than outside, climbing trees or spraying each other with water or tossing baseballs back and forth, but that's how it was.

I don't think Tommy would have wanted to do those things anyway. After all, he wasn't a regular kid. Weird is what I would have called him, if I hadn't known about his autism.

Grandma also finally got around to telling me how Billy Bones had died. I'd spent a week imagining something spectacular and awful. He'd been a hero, jumping in a river to save a drowning kid, or he'd fought off some robbers, or else he'd stood up to mean white folks who were trying to force some innocent black people out of their homes.

"It was just a dumb car accident," she said. "It was late one night. He and his band were driving to the next town, where they were booked to play the following night.

He was sleeping in the back seat. The driver had had a few glasses of beer before taking off. Maybe he was even drinking along the way. We'll never know. Anyway, he missed a turn and the car went off the road, then crashed into a tree. Everyone got off with scrapes and cuts. Everyone except your grandpa. He was thrown out of the car. Didn't have a mark on him. In fact, they kept expecting him to open his eyes and yell 'Boo.' But his neck was broken. He died instantly. And that was that."

She didn't cry when she told me about it. After all these years, I suppose she had long ago run out of tears.

"What year was that?"

Grandma didn't hesitate. "1938," she said.

I thought about all those magazines in the basement and how the issues stopped in 1938. Now it all made sense. When Billy Bones died, a part of Grandma had died with him.

A week or so after Tommy had brought the trombone downstairs, Grandma and I made our usual stop at the market for fresh bread and peanut butter.

But instead of taking one of our usual routes back home, Grandma led me in the other direction. "Where are we going?" I asked, licking peanut butter off my fingers. "Home is thataway."

"You'll find out soon enough."

Halfway down a strange block, she stopped, squinting up at the line of shop signs hanging above the building entrances.

"I *think* this is the right place," she said, frowning. "I'm looking for Oscar's Music Store. Do you see it, Maya?"

I looked in the direction she was facing, and then I turned in a circle, noticing the battered sign across the street— SCAR'S MUSIC STOR —missing the first and last letters.

"Over there," I said, pointing.

"Lead the way," Grandma ordered.

We went up to the corner, crossed the street with the light, and then backtracked down the other side. I held open the faded green door to the music store for Grandma.

"Thank you," she said, ever polite. She halted just inside the entrance, scanning the dim interior. I could hear music playing softly somewhere. The walls were decorated with dusty musical instruments. There were trombones and trumpets and a half dozen others that I couldn't identify. A couple of long shelves dominated the interior, stacked haphazardly with an assortment of boxes and musical accessories. Looking down an aisle, I could see a glass case along the back wall and a cash register sitting on top of it.

"Oscar?" Grandma yelled. "You dead yet?"

I heard the music stop, a door open and close.

"Oscar? That you or your ghost?"

I heard a laugh as a tall black man appeared behind the glass case. He disappeared from sight for a moment as he found his way around it, and then reappeared again as he came down the aisle toward us.

"Ruby St. Clair!" he exclaimed in a voice that rattled the windows. "Ain't you a sight for sore eyes." He grabbed her firmly by the waist and kissed her on the cheek.

I'm not sure what surprised me more—that he kissed her or that she let him.

Oscar stared warmly at my grandma for a moment, while she transformed before my eyes into someone shy and girlish. Underneath her makeup, I could even see the blush in her cheeks.

"Nice to see you, too, Oscar," Grandma said, breaking the spell. "Let me introduce my granddaughter. Maya, this is Mr. Oscar Parker."

Mr. Parker looked at me, his eyebrows arching with surprise. "My, my," he said, suddenly beaming with pleasure. "I am mighty pleased to meet you, Maya."

I was relieved when he just offered his hand for me to shake. I'm not sure what I would have done if he had tried to kiss me on the cheek.

"She's staying with me this summer," Grandma said.

"So you just happened to be walking by and thought the friendly thing to do would be to step on in and introduce her to an old friend?" Mr. Parker asked, chuckling.

"Well, no," Grandma replied tartly.

"That's my Ruby," Mr. Parker said, leaning down close and talking to me as if we were a couple of long-lost buddies. "She was never one to use five words when two will do."

"It's called brevity, Mr. Parker," Grandma interjected.

"You see, Maya," Mr. Parker continued, without skipping a beat, "I've always had a thing for your grandma. In fact, we all once played in a band together. My, your grandma sang like nobody else. If your grandpa hadn't beat me to the punch, I think I would have gone and married her myself."

"Makes me sound like an old bone that a couple of dogs were fighting over," interrupted my grandma. But I could see that she liked the attention. Her eyes were sparkling, her face open and beautiful.

"So then, if it isn't a desperate need to see me again, what brings you all the way uptown to my place?"

"Maya's started playing Billy's horn," Grandma said.

"That so?" Mr. Parker said.

I nodded.

"Most girls nowadays want to play the guitar," Mr. Parker said, with a sigh. "All that rock and roll and hippie music. The rest want to play flutes made out of bamboo, or seaweed, or somethin'. Are you sure you like somethin' as old-fashioned as a trombone?"

"I don't really care what other girls like to play," I said, lifting my chin.

Mr. Parker looked me over as if I were a grapefruit or a lawnmower. "I suppose she just might have enough spunk to play trombone."

"Do you still offer lessons," Grandma asked, "or is that something you've given up because you're just too darn lazy?"

"Whoo-ee," Mr. Parker chuckled. "You see, Maya, that's where you get yer spitfire." He pointed at my grandma. "That's one of the things I always loved about you, Ruby."

"You can save your sweet talk for your girlfriends. So, what about it?"

"Yes'm. I'm still giving lessons. But only to people that are special. You special, Maya?"

I remember staring open-mouthed back at Mr. Parker. Lessons? Grandma hadn't said another word about them. "What was that?" I said, stalling for time.

"He asked if you were a special child," Grandma said.

I didn't hesitate. "You bet I am," I said fiercely.

# Chapter Twenty-Two

Two days later, I started trombone lessons with Mr. Oscar Parker, the well-known bebop tenor saxophone player, occasional trombonist, sometime music store owner, and longtime admirer of my grandmother.

Lessons were every Wednesday and Friday afternoon, right after lunch. We would walk over to Oscar's Music Store, stopping by the market for a quick bite of lunch. Grandma would sit outside or do an errand or two while I took my half-hour lesson in one of the small, dingy practice rooms at the back of the shop.

"I played with ol' Billy," Oscar said during my first lesson. "Bet you don't know that we go way back to when we were just barefoot kids in Oklahoma. There were the three of us—Billy, Ruby, and me—all from the same no-name, godforsaken town. Billy was a mighty fine 'bone player," he said, with a shake of his head. "One of the best. The sounds his horn and my tenor sax could make, whooeee! Sometimes it was about as good as it can get this side of heaven."

"I never met him," I said.

"I suppose you didn't," Mr. Parker remarked, "but now you're playing his horn."

I nodded.

"Well, then, I'd say it ain't like you never met him. You're just goin' to meet him in a different way, through his music and his horn. Ready to get started?"

"Yes," was all I said, not realizing what his words really meant.

Playing the trombone is more difficult than it sounds. Instead of just worrying about my fingers hitting the right keys, like with the piano, I had to make sure my lips were set in just the right position. Too tight and the note would come out too high. Too loose and the note might be too low or it might not be a note at all, sounding more like the call of some strange, sick beast. There were no marks on the slide, so it was hard to know how far out—or in—to move it.

"Hear the note in your mind first," Oscar would say, singing out a tone. "And then move your slide to match it."

At first, I couldn't do it at all. But miraculously, by the end of the first lesson, I was able to play a simple song.

Sure, it was only "Three Blind Mice," but it was a song and I was playing it. I considered it a victory.

172

"What do you think, Oscar?" Grandma asked when we were done.

Mr. Parker patted me on the head affectionately and said, "She's a special one. Like you and Billy Bones. You were right to bring her."

I was surprised at how his words made me feel. Suddenly warm and wonderful and, yes—that was it—special.

I had always done okay in school, and I had played piano long enough to become pretty good at it, though I knew I could never, ever be as good as Tommy. But the trombone—why, it was as if I had been waiting my whole life to discover it. And now, here was a grown-up saying I was special—and meaning it.

Of course, the lessons weren't free. I found that out soon enough. And Grandma had no intention of paying for them, either. I found that out soon enough, too.

But Mr. Parker liked having a clean car. And I didn't mind washing cars, so we struck a deal. In exchange for lessons twice a week, I agreed to wash Mr. Parker's car once a week. I figured I was coming out on the good end of the deal, assuming, for some reason, that he'd drive a car like my mom's, a tiny little 1965 Volkswagen Bug.

I should have known better from the way he grinned when we shook hands.

A few hours after my first lesson, I was startled from

my chair by a loud blast from a car horn. I glanced out the front window and saw a huge Cadillac convertible pulled up next to the curb. It was so dirty, it was hard to tell its true color. Oscar was leaning against the fender, arms folded, enjoying the evening sunshine.

"Mr. Parker's here," I heard Grandma sing out. "Sponges, bucket, and soap are under the kitchen sink."

"I know, I know—" I yelled back.

Over the following weeks, I never saw Mr. Parker's Cadillac that dirty again. Not even close.

"Nice job on my car, Maya," Mr. Parker said at the start of my next lesson.

"You're welcome," I replied.

We spent the rest of the time listening to records, Mr. Parker pointing out notes and phrases and sounds.

"Most musicians don't listen enough," he said. "They practice, practice, practice, but sometimes you just need to sit your bottom down and listen. That's the only way you gonna get better. By listening."

At first, it all sounded horribly complicated to me. But slowly, by the end of our first session, I began to hear some of the things he wanted me to hear. Maybe it was Oscar's influence or that old ghost of my grandpa, Billy Bones, possessing me. Or maybe I'd finally found something I really loved, something I was just meant to do.

Grandma was waiting for me when the lesson was over. Oscar's eyes lit up when he saw her. "Say, you're just the lady I wanted to talk to."

"Uh-hummm," Grandma replied in a tone that said she didn't believe a word of it.

"No, honest," Oscar protested. "We're having a special benefit concert at the club. It's for the Retired Jazz Musicians' Fund. Six weeks from Friday night. I'm hoping I can coax you back onstage."

I gave my grandma a stare. "Stage?" I said.

Grandma frowned in Oscar's direction. "You know I don't sing anymore," she snipped. "I gave all that up years ago."

"But what about the church choir?" I reminded her.

"Shush," Grandma warned. "That isn't the same thing."

"You sly gal," Oscar said, with a chuckle. "I shoulda known that you couldn't give it up. You just switched to singin' for that cat—what's his name?—ah, yes, now I remember, Count Jesus. Come on, Ruby. It's for a good cause. It ain't like the wild old days."

"They weren't all that wild," she said, glaring at me. "I don't want you to give Maya the wrong idea."

"So you were a jazz singer?" I said, another piece added to my family puzzle.

"She coulda been a great one," Oscar quipped. "Ella, Billie . . . Ruby."

I gave Grandma a hard look. She still seemed like the same old grandma, but somehow, knowing that she had been a jazz singer long ago made me see her differently. That image of her as a young woman, standing in a spotlight on a stage, singing to a room full of people, merged with the woman I had come to know. It was like looking in a glass prism and turning it ever so slowly, watching how the colors change and shimmer, even though the prism itself stays the same.

Grandma gave an embarrassed laugh. "Go on, Oscar. I was never that good."

"Sure you won't reconsider, Ruby? We'd love to have you, and it would mean a lot to me and some of the other boys to play with you again."

"You're very kind, Oscar, but I'm sorry to say that I'm about as likely to sing in a club again as you are to be sitting in the front pew at a house of the Lord next Sunday morning."

It took Oscar four quick strides before he was standing in front of her. He held out his hand. Grandma looked up at him, puzzled, and then took it.

"Miz Ruby St. Clair, you have yourself a deal. And since you're a devout, God-fearing woman, I expect you to keep up your end of the bargain."

Grandma snatched back her hand. "You in church? That'll be the day." She did a quick pivot and headed out of the shop, slamming the door after her.

I stifled a giggle. "See you at church."

"Already lookin' forward to it," Oscar replied, with a soft chuckle. "And keep an eye on that grandma of yours."

You can imagine Grandma's surprise that next Sunday morning when we rounded the last corner and spied that bright red, freshly scrubbed Cadillac convertible parked next to the curb right in front of the Mt. Zion Holy Baptist Tabernacle and Church of God.

I felt her hesitate and almost turn back toward home, but Oscar spied us and stopped us in our tracks. "Good mornin', ladies," his voice boomed, turning heads up and down the street. "I've been waitin' for y'all."

To her credit, Grandma pasted a smile on her face and forged onward.

Oscar hopped off the fender as we approached.

"Good morning, Mr. Parker," Grandma said. "A little early for you, isn't it?"

"Or awful late," Oscar yawned, offering my grandma one arm and me the other. "But it was worth it just to see the look on your face a moment ago."

"Oh, shush," my grandma said.

"I hope you don't mind me escorting the two most beautiful women in Seattle into church."

Before Grandma could make another smart comment, I answered for both of us. "Not at all," I said, with a giggle.

Oscar made a grand entrance, leading us right down the center aisle. He nodded and smiled greetings along the way. I was surprised at how many men and women he seemed to know by name. For somebody who never came to church, he sure seemed to be friendly with a lot of churchgoers.

After the sermon, he stayed with us in line, waiting his turn to greet Reverend Gillespie, who was standing by the front door. They hugged each other like long-lost friends.

"Hope to see you here again, Oscar," Reverend Gillespie said.

"You can thank Ruby for this time," Oscar said.

"How's that?" Reverend Gillespie said.

"She's agreed to sing at a club again," I couldn't help chirping.

I saw my grandma tense, and Reverend Gillespie's grin seemed to lose some of its warmth. He tucked his double chin into his chest, but before he could say anything, Oscar stepped in, smooth as could be. "Don't worry, Del. It ain't like that. We had a little deal. I come to church, and she agrees to sing again at a charity event. It's for retired jazz musicians living here in town. We're just hoping to help them out by raisin' a little money."

Reverend Gillespie thought for a moment and then nodded his approval. "A worthy cause," he announced. "Thank you for lending your talents, Sistah St. Clair."

"Not at all," Grandma said stiffly.

And that was that.

"Can I give you a ride home?" Oscar offered.

I eyed the bright red Cadillac with white leather interior and rocket fins on the back corners. It was easy to imagine myself in the back seat, waving to the Garcias as we drove by.

"Neatly done, Oscar," Grandma said. "I have to give you that."

"I just didn't want you to change your mind," Oscar said, with a chuckle.

"No fear of that now," Grandma sighed. "Lord, what am I going to sing?"

"Not sure the Almighty will have any suggestions," Oscar said, "but I'd say pick something pretty. No doubt about it. Hop in?"

Grandma shook her head. "I think we could use the exercise."

Oscar nodded. "Suit yourself. I do appreciate your agreeing to sing." And then he provided fuel for a month of gossip by giving her a kiss on the cheek—right there on the front steps of the church.

Grandma was still blushing when Oscar tooted his car horn and roared off down the street.

"He's sweet on you, Grandma," I said.

"Oh, shush," she exclaimed.

# Chapter Twenty-Three

The six-inch bundle of letters on the mat outside the front door was bound tightly by a rubber band. Too thick to push through the mail slot, the mail carrier had just left them there on the doorstep.

I raced ahead of my grandma, my heart pounding with excitement, and snatched them off the ground. I had known it all along. I was right, and everyone else had been wrong. Dad was okay, he was safe! It was just the mail, that was all. Someone had finally found all of his letters that had been lost and then forwarded them all to me in one big, wonderful bunch.

"What is it, Maya?" Grandma asked, puffing up the steps after me.

The envelope on the top of the stack was bruised and battered from all the handling. It wasn't enough, however, to hide the address. I looked closely and then blinked.

It didn't make sense. I tore off the rubber band and

began frantically thumbing through the rest of the letters. They were all addressed to the same person: Master Sergeant James Thompson. My dad. They also all had the same words stamped across the front: RETURN TO SENDER.

My mouth was dry. "Nothing," I finally said. "It's nothing."

"What's wrong?"

"There's been a mistake," I said.

"What kind of mistake?"

"These letters to my dad," I said, voice rising, waving them in front of her face. "Those stupid, stupid people. See, see here? Every one of them says 'Return to Sender,' like I'm just some nobody who doesn't know any better. But see, I know his address. I would never get that wrong! He's been counting on these letters. Expecting to get them from me. How's he going to know that I care about him, if those stupid idiots didn't deliver them to him? Don't they know he's in Vietnam? They sent him there, didn't they? They were the ones. And they messed up."

"Oh, Maya," Grandma said, moving to gather me in her arms.

I would have none of it. I took a step back, shaking my head. After all, she was one of them. She'd never believed in him. She'd as much as admitted it just after I arrived. And everything that had happened over the past weeks, the way I was beginning to feel about her, it all had been a lie.

"I'm going to call a general or something," I yelled. "Or maybe that Walter Cronkite on the news. Maybe he can figure out what's wrong and why my dad can't get his mail."

"But Maya, your daddy is—"

"No, don't you say it!" I began wailing, my face red with emotion. I waved the letters at her, tears streaming down my face. "I'll hate you if you say it, just like I hate my mom for saying it."

"Honey, your daddy is missing in action," Grandma said firmly. "You know that. He's been lost for six months now. They don't know what has become of him. They can't deliver your letters. They don't know where he is—"

My cry of agony cut her off. "But I know, I know. He's in South Vietnam. He's not lost. That's where he is. And he's coming home, he's coming home real soon. And when that happens, I'm leaving here. He's not missing. He's not DEAD!"

There it was, the word I had been dreading for months and months. And because of Grandma, I had been forced to say it out loud. As soon as I heard that word, I knew it had to be true, knew it in my heart. He wasn't just missing, he was gone. Dead. Saying that word made it real as surely as if I had killed him myself.

Grandma took another step toward me, but I whirled around, dashed into the house and raced up the stairs, all those letters to Master Sergeant James Thompson slipping from my hand and scattering in my wake.

Grandma didn't follow me up. She left me alone. As I lay on my mom's old bed, watching the patch of sunlight arc across the room, I slowly went over the events of the past weeks and months, playing them back over and over in my mind like an old movie. Then as the light began to fade, I realized what I had to do.

It was time to go.

I waited until it was dark, half listening as Grandma came upstairs, paused at my door, and then shuffled down the hallway. I heard her in the bathroom, saw the light underneath my door snuff out, and then heard the door to her room click shut. I waited another hour, lying motionless on the bed, barely breathing.

And then it was time to leave. There wasn't much to do. I suppose I had been ready from the first moment I got there.

I thought about leaving a note, but as I stood over my mom's old desk, staring at a blank sheet of paper, I realized that I didn't have anything to say. I guess my grandmother was still a stranger after all.

And now, so was I. I didn't need my mom, and I didn't need Grandma.

I slipped silently out the front door, roughly pushing Harry S. Truman back as he tried to follow me out the door. I hurried down the steps, turned left at the sidewalk, and trotted down the dark, silent street toward downtown.

The bus station was just as I remembered it. There was the same line of taxis, and a crowd of buses was waiting in the huge parking lot.

I pushed through the glass doors and then walked briskly across the worn tile floor toward the ticket counter on the far wall. I stopped at a dirty red line on the floor, right next to a sign that said "Wait here."

I waited.

And waited.

And waited some more.

I watched the minute hand creep past five minutes. When it hit seven minutes, I figured the man at the counter must not have seen me standing there. I cleared my throat.

The ticket agent still didn't look up, but it was enough to get his attention. "Next?" he said, his voice sounding scratchy and rough as an old nail file.

I stepped up to the counter, cringing at the squeak, squeak, squeak my sneakers made on the floor.

"I'd like a ticket please," I said.

"Where to?"

"Oh, uh, Chicago."

"One way or round trip?" The words tumbled out so easily I figured he must have said them ten thousand times. Maybe I was ten thousand and one. Lucky me.

"One way."

"Forty-nine dollars."

"Excuse me?" I couldn't help it. The words had sneaked out before I had a chance to take them back. I had only the money I'd taken from my mom. $38.53. It wasn't enough.

"How about Los Angeles, then?" I said quickly.

Slow as a turtle, the ticket agent's chin came up until his eyes were no longer staring at the countertop, but were looking down at me. He had a long nose, each nostril choked with more hair than was visible anywhere else on his head. His gray eyes were magnified by glasses with lenses as thick as the bottom of a Coke bottle.

"Now, which is it? Chicago or Los Angeles?" He glanced left and right. "Say, how old are you, darling?" he drawled, flashing me a yellow-toothed smile.

"Thir—I mean, fifteen," I said stiffly, not liking the way he said "darling."

"Fifteen," he said softly, looking at me in a way that

made me want to walk up and slug him in the nose. "Nah. If you're fifteen, darling, then I'm Ringo Starr. Say, where's your mother?"

"Uh, she's in the bathroom," I said, holding back a shiver.

I'd been warm enough when I was walking, but now that I was standing there, I was cold and getting colder.

"Uh-huh," he said. "Wait there." He looked over his shoulder. "Bud," I heard him say, "I think we got ourselves a sweet one."

This wasn't going the way I had planned. I took one step back and slid behind a tall black man hurrying toward the door. "Wait up, daddy," I said in a singsong voice as I followed him outside. He didn't even notice I was behind him. When he turned right, I turned left. I had no idea where I was going next.

At first, I didn't notice her sitting on the bench outside the door. But then she spoke: "Sit down!" I nearly jumped with surprise. Grandma waited for her words to sink in, and then she added, "Please, Maya."

My jaw must have dropped all the way to the top of my sneakers before bouncing back up. I hesitated a moment, glancing over my shoulder at the street beyond, part of me thinking about running, running, and never, ever stopping. But then I pulled off my backpack and collapsed on the far end of the bench, feeling more miserable and mixed up than I had ever felt before.

"Chicago is a nice enough city," she said. "I spent some time there once long ago."

"How did you know?" I'm sure my voice sounded sullen, the anger from weeks earlier rushing back like it had never really gone away.

Grandma just stared at me. "Give me a little credit, dear," she said quietly. "I saw where you were sending your letters. I put two and two together. I must confess, though, that I was worried you were going to run off earlier in the summer. The first two weeks you were here, I don't think I slept much at night, expecting you to try."

Right about then, I noticed the creepy ticket agent staring out the door. Something about his presence made Grandma look up. She skewered him with a glare. I saw him glance at me with something like disappointment, look at her again, and then jerk his head back inside like a bug looking for cover.

"Pervert," I muttered.

"What was that?" Grandma said.

"That ticket agent. I didn't—"

Grandma raised her hand. "Tut, tut, tut," she clucked. "I was standing near enough at the start to have some idea of the game he was playing and hear what you said. Now, what are you going to do?"

"What do you mean?"

"I am prepared to buy you a ticket to Chicago and send you on your way. Elizabeth's mother convinced your mother to agree to it a few weeks after you arrived."

"Nobody mentioned anything to me about it."

Grandma ignored my comment. "Of course, if it was me, I would go to Florida. Always wanted to join a circus. I thought it would be fun to make cotton candy or run an arcade. If I were running away for the summer, I can't imagine a more delightful place to be."

"You'd really let me go?"

Grandma didn't say a word.

I settled against the back of the bench and dropped my chin to my chest, my heart pounding away.

"But before you decide," Grandma said, "I have a few things I want to say." I noticed now that her voice was shaking. "First of all, I want you to know that I'm sorry that you couldn't stay home for the summer. It must have been hard to come to a strange place to live with a stranger. I have lived alone for so long, I know I didn't do a very good job of making you feel wanted when you first arrived.

"I'm also sorry that your daddy was sent to Vietnam. And I can't tell you how sorry I am that he is missing. I know you think otherwise, but pretending something isn't so does not change anything. As much as I wanted Billy to be alive, as many times as I imagined him walking up those front steps and taking me in his arms, it didn't ever change what happened.

"But mostly, I'm sorry I let so much time pass without getting to know you. You cannot imagine how excited I was to have you coming to spend the summer with me. It was a gift. But I didn't want to force anything. Goodness knows I'm a stranger to you, but I was hoping for a chance to get to know my only granddaughter. And I wanted a chance, perhaps the last chance, to mend fences that were too long broken. But I cannot do the mending by myself. I need you to help me.

"Of course, I won't stop you from going to Chicago. But I hope you will change your mind and stay with me until it's time to go home. It's just a few more weeks. Maybe this is all too heavy a burden for a thirteen-year-old girl, but that's the way it is.

"Maya, no one ever promised that life was going to be fair. You have to decide what you're going to do and how you're going to be. It's all up to you."

Those last words seemed to shimmer in the air between us: it was all up to me.

"Grandma, I . . ." I could not get another word out. I felt like crying all over again, but I vowed that I was past tears. I stared at my shoes and shivered. All the hurt and anger of the past weeks and months seemed to have burned away, leaving behind a big, charred, hollow space in my soul. Dad was not missing in action; he was not a prisoner of war, either. I knew he was never coming back.

"I guess I'll stay." I suddenly felt more tired than I had ever felt before. "I guess I'll stay."

"You guess?"

"I'll stay," I said more forcefully.

"Are you sure?"

"Yes."

"Okay, baby," Grandma said, satisfied for the moment. "Let's go home."

I didn't want to move. I just wanted to lie down right there and sleep for a few years. "I don't think I can make it," I sighed.

"Sure you can," Grandma said. "You are much stronger than you can ever imagine."

Then she helped me to my feet, an old woman helping a teenage girl. Must have looked mighty strange to somebody watching us. But that wasn't half of it.

On our way past the buses, Grandma stopped next to a man built like a football player and made even more imposing by an explosion of hair. He had the largest Afro I had ever seen. While he was unloading luggage from the belly of a recently arrived bus and stacking it onto a cart, she whispered a few words into his ear. I managed to over-hear her say "ticket agent."

He nodded once and then glanced at the entrance to the bus station, wiping his hands on the front of his stained coveralls. "I know who you mean," he said, his mouth stretching into a thin smile. "I'll take care of him for you, Miz St. Clair," he rumbled. "See you on Sunday." He patted me on the shoulder with a hand the size of a catcher's mitt. Nobody needed to spell out what "I'll take care of him" meant.

As we walked along, the night cool and dark, the full weight of what had just happened began to press down on me. I staggered while crossing a street. I would have fallen to my knees, but Grandma grabbed me tight and helped me keep going.

I suppose walking back home was the right thing to do. I needed to keep moving. It would have been easy to give up on everything at that point. And Grandma knew that.

That walk is still one of the hardest things I've ever done. I was still in Seattle. Dad was gone forever. Nothing had changed—except my whole life.

Just before we turned onto Grandma's street, I felt something change inside of me. Just a flutter of warmth, as if a small ember had come back to life. Maybe it had never completely died out.

"You know, this doesn't mean we're friends or anything," I said softly.

Grandma didn't even break stride.

"I didn't expect it would, child," she replied. "I didn't expect it at all."

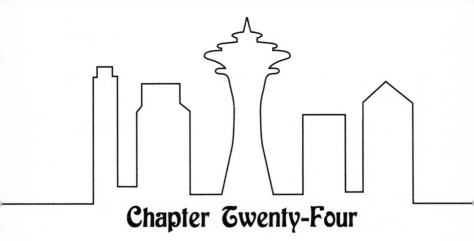

# Chapter Twenty-Four

August was a surprise. This was supposed to be the Northwest. That meant cold, wet winters and, well, cold, wet summers, too. Yet day after day dawned clear and warm, and it got even warmer with each passing day.

After working in the morning, Grandma and I would usually seek relief by taking the bus to Seward Park on Lake Washington.

Grandma would sit in a chair in the shade, reading a book with her magnifying glass, while I swam in the water or wandered up and down the beach.

It was fun enough, but I kept wishing that my best friend Elizabeth were there. Even Tommy would have been good company, but unfortunately, he was terrified of the lake and wasn't all that fond of a bathtub full of water, either, according to Mrs. Richards.

One afternoon when it wasn't so hot, we decided to skip the lake. Grandma wasn't feeling well, so she was in her room napping.

Because of the heat, I'd been practicing the trombone in the evening. But that left an afternoon with nothing to do. I'd decided to make cookies, and Harry S. Truman was keeping me company.

I heard a soft knock on the back door. "Come on in, Tommy," I yelled.

There was another knock. "Come on in," I yelled again. "Don't start acting normal on me now."

I heard the screen door creak open, looked up, and let out a yelp of surprise.

He stood in the doorway, holding his hat in his hand. An elderly black man, he was hardly any taller than me. His face was shiny wet with sweat, and he kept wiping it with a soggy red handkerchief.

"'Scuse me, missy, but I was lookin' for Miz Ruby St. Clair."

It took me just a moment to recover from my fright. "I thought you were somebody else," I said accusingly.

"Nope, it's just me," the man said, a soft smile playing across his lips.

That's when I recognized him. "I know you," I said, pointing a finger at him. "You were playing that day on the street."

"Yes'm, that's right," he said, nodding and wiping his face again.

"And Grandma invited you up to the house."

"That's right, too," he said. "But I see she ain't 'round, so I think I'll be goin'."

He began to back out through the door, but I rushed forward, grabbed him by the hand, and pulled him into the kitchen.

"No, sir," I said. "Grandma is just taking a little rest. You sit right here. Let me get you a glass of water, Mister . . . ?"

"Johnson. Sonny Ray."

"Okay, Mr. Johnson. Grandma will be really upset if you leave without her getting a chance to say hello." I set the glass down in front of him. He drank greedily, then looked up for more.

"How about some lemonade this time?" I asked.

He gave me a bright smile, and that's when it occurred to me that this might be a chance to learn more about Grandma without her around to object or change the subject.

My cookies weren't done yet, but Grandma had made a blackberry pie that morning. "Can I get you some pie, Mr. Johnson, with a scoop of ice cream on top?" I said in my sweetest voice.

"That'd be just lovely," he replied.

I slid the plate in front of him. He tucked the napkin

into his shirt collar. The way he dove into that pie, I realized it must have been a long time since he had tasted something homemade that was so good.

"That's the best pie I ever did eat," he said, when he'd finished his second piece. He pushed the plate away and groaned with pleasure.

"Your grandma is a real sleeper," he commented.

"She wasn't feelin' well," I said. "I'll go get her in a minute. So you and her were friends from way back?"

"Ruby has a lot of friends from way back," Mr. Johnson said. "Say, you wouldn't have no toothpick handy? I got a blackberry seed stuck."

It took me a minute to find them.

He worked with the toothpick for a moment, pried out the seed, and then continued. "Yes. I knew her from a long time ago, and Billy, too. Your grandma, she cut quite a figure back then. Purtiest girl around. And that voice! My, oh my. I swear that she woulda made Ella and Billie jealous if she'd a kept at it."

"You didn't tell me we had company."

Mr. Johnson was already getting to his feet. "Nice to see you again, Ruby. Feelin' better?"

"Yes," Grandma said, giving me a sharp eye. "I see my granddaughter has been taking care of you."

"Oh, yes. Polite girl. Well-mannered. She loaded me

down with pie, lemonade, and water. And now we were just talkin'."

"About me, it sounds like," Grandma interrupted.

Mr. Johnson gave her one of his big, wide grins. "Why, I think you be a tad embarrassed by it all."

Grandma pulled up a chair and sat down, and that's when I finally learned how she and Billy Bones and Mr. Johnson had met. Turns out Grandma, Mr. Johnson, and Billy all lived within 50 miles of each other. They didn't get acquainted until they entered a music contest sponsored by a local radio station and swept the first three places. I also learned why she had turned her back on singing.

"Why did you stop?" I asked her.

"I didn't want that kind of life," she replied. "Simple as that. Working nights, sleeping out of a car, never getting decent food, putting up with the kind of people you wouldn't let through your front door. I loved the music, sure enough; I just didn't love the rest of it."

"And Grandpa?"

"Oh, he was a special one," Grandma said. "Didn't seem to bother him none. He could eat just about anything. Sleep like a baby anywhere."

"We all had to make a livin'," Mr. Johnson added with a shrug. "That means you put up with all the other—"

"Sonny Ray Johnson!" my grandmother warned.

"Stuff," Mr. Johnson finished. "Ladies present. I know'd that."

Grandma sent Mr. Sonny Ray Johnson home a few hours later with the rest of the pie, enough food for a week, and a promise to visit again very soon.

That night, I asked Grandma how it had been, singing with Billy Bones.

"What do you think?"

I shrugged. "Groovy?"

"I think that about covers it," she whispered.

# Chapter Twenty-Five

About a week or so after Mr. Sonny Ray Johnson's visit, I was sitting on the front steps of the library, waiting for Grandma to finish up with her work. I had a bag full of books, but I didn't feel like looking at any of them just then.

Besides, what was happening on the streets that day was much more interesting than any book. Grandma had warned me about staying close. "Sometime today, there may be a lot of people on the street," she said. "When that happens, you come find me. Got it?"

I'd responded with a nod. But she wasn't telling me anything I didn't already know. My friends at Students for a Free America had warned me about what was coming, and I had no intention of leaving my perch now. In fact, I was hoping to see some of them carrying my signs.

It turned out that I wasn't the only one who was angry for most of that summer. There were lots and lots of people upset about the war in Vietnam. And I had become one of them.

I watched as the crowds on the sidewalks suddenly thinned. Then, the sidewalks began to fill with a surge of people. I had always enjoyed people watching, but this time it was different. The faces of everyone I saw—moms in dresses, longhaired kids in tie-dyed T-shirts, old women clutching their purses to their chests as they scurried away—all shared one thing: fear.

I ran up to the top of the steps to get a better look, dragging my backpack behind me. There was a growing roar down the street to my left, followed by muffled explosions that sounded like cars backfiring. And then the roar was transformed into angry shouts, and a disorganized mob was backing around the corner and was being pushed in my direction. I saw a few people flinging rocks and bottles. Their targets were a row of dark blue uniforms stretching across the street—the police. They wore helmets and held shields in front of them, like Roman warriors in history books. But instead of spears, they had long batons that they flicked into the crowd when anyone got too close.

I remembered my grandma's orders, but my knees began to quiver and I remained rooted to the spot, too fascinated to move.

Then a lot of things happened all at once.

There was a faint whistle, and the line of police on foot suddenly parted in the middle, letting about a dozen police on horseback pass though. At the sight of the horses, the demonstrators began to run.

I don't know what directed my eye to that specific spot on the sidewalk. But there he was, Mr. Sonny Ray Johnson, standing across the street, clinging to a parking meter as all the chaos swirled around him like white water around a river rock.

But he was no rock, and the look on his face left me with no choice. I knew what I had to do.

I bolted down the steps toward him.

"Maya!" Grandma screamed, coming outside too late to stop me. I didn't pause or think or do anything but head straight toward Mr. Johnson.

I still had my backpack filled with books, and I remember using it once, swinging it like a club when a young wild-haired man almost ran me over.

And then I was beside him. "Mr. Johnson? It's me, Maya," I said, gasping for breath. "Please. We gotta go."

Mr. Johnson's eyes were open, but I could tell he was somewhere else. I tugged at his coat. When he didn't respond, I took his hands, pried them off the parking meter, and then started pulling him back across the street toward the library.

I knew I had to get him out of danger, and the library seemed like the safest place.

He didn't resist. I'm not sure what I would have done if he had refused to move, but he followed me like a child. By now, the crowd had begun to thin, leaving only the angriest demonstrators. They retreated like guerilla fighters, running back a few yards, pulling bottles or rocks out of their backpacks, then throwing them at the advancing police.

There were more explosions. White clouds drifted toward us, making me cough and my eyes water.

"Don't worry, Mr. Johnson," I sputtered, hoping I sounded more confident than I felt. "We're almost there."

At one point, I slipped, skinning my knee. But I was back on my feet in a second, never letting go of Mr. Johnson's hand.

And then came the moment that made Mr. Johnson and me famous, at least for a day or two.

We were almost to the other side of the street when a huge horse appeared. I knew all about the Trojan horse, and this one seemed at least that gigantic.

The monster was charging right at us, its eyes white with excitement, its black coat shiny with sweat, and I knew we couldn't get out of the way in time.

But instead of closing my eyes, I did just the opposite, even though I was scared to death. When the horse was almost on top of us, I whirled my backpack and flung it at the horse, screaming with all the fear, fury, and rage I'd been carrying inside me all summer.

I screamed in defiance of whatever memories were terrorizing Mr. Johnson.

I screamed for my dad and all the others who were killed, maimed, and lost in that stupid, foolish war.

And I screamed for myself because, well, I was terrified.

That's when a photographer for the local newspaper took our picture—a defiant black girl holding the hand of an elderly, gentle-looking but terrified black man. The next day, it would be in newspapers across the country.

In the end, I didn't even know what had finally done it. Well, I like to think it was my scream, but it was probably the books spilling out of my backpack and appearing like a flock of birds in that giant horse's path. The horse, startled, stopped short, its forelegs stiff as it skidded to a halt right in front of me—instead of charging right over us and flattening us both.

I was so relieved that I almost kissed that horse right on the nose—that's how close it came.

A moment later, we were up the steps, Grandma grabbing us and hustling us into the library and back to her office.

"It was Mr. Johnson," I said.

"Oh, Lord, I know, I know," she said, grabbing me by the shoulders. "Scared me half to death and beyond. I don't know whether to switch you or hug you."

She decided on a fierce hug. Then she turned to Mr. Johnson, who was just standing there, all limp and lost.

"Ruby? I wet myself," he whispered, plucking at the front of his trousers. "I couldn't help it. I was back there. I was back there all over again."

"You're safe now, Sonny Ray," Grandma said. "I'd a wet myself too, if I'd a been caught in the middle of all that commotion. Now, let's get you cleaned up." Grandma was back in charge. "Maya, go downstairs and find Mr. Stachofsky. He takes care of the building. Get some coveralls from him. Tell him I sent you."

"Yes'm," I said.

I found Mr. Stachofsky after ten minutes of looking, and with some creative explaining—after all, I didn't want to embarrass Mr. Johnson by telling everyone that he'd peed himself—I convinced him to lend me some old denim coveralls. Mr. Johnson was in the bathroom upstairs, with Grandma standing guard outside. She flagged me down, then passed the coveralls in through the door.

Mr. Johnson shuffled out a little later, carrying a bag that contained his soiled trousers under one arm. Humiliated, he would not look at either of us.

Acting on a sudden inspiration, I spoke to him. "I appreciate you saving me and all, Mr. Johnson," I said, grabbing his hand and squeezing it tight.

"Wha—what's that?" he said.

"I don't know what made me run out into all that trouble. I'm just glad you were there to rescue me."

Mr. Johnson's face wrinkled with confusion.

"I did what?" he said, more to himself than to me. "I don' remember much of anythin', to be truthful."

"You saved me," I said fervently. "Thanks, Mr. Johnson."

His face softened into a confused grin. "You're welcome," he said. "I was most glad t' be of service."

Over Mr. Johnson's shoulder, Grandma nodded, smiling.

Of course, I wouldn't consider letting Mr. Johnson go home. In fact, I made Grandma talk the library director into driving us all back home right away.

Mr. Johnson protested about it not being proper and all, but I wouldn't hear any of it. Thank goodness, neither would Grandma.

"Maya's right," she said. "There's a room in the basement for you. It's yours for as long as you want it."

Later that same evening, after Mr. Johnson had gone to bed, Grandma told me about the race riots that had raged in other parts of the country when she was not much older than I was. She explained that entire neighborhoods, houses, and businesses were destroyed and that many black folks, including children, were killed out of spite, hatred, and pure evil.

Even more horrible, my great-grandfather was one of them. His death, along with all the other terrible things that had happened, was what drove Grandma, Billy Bones, Sonny Ray, Oscar, and countless others to move north and west, away from so much tragedy and trouble.

"I understand now," I said when Grandma was done.

"I don't think you do," she replied, her eyes black as obsidian and just as hard. "And it's better that you don't."

# Chapter Twenty-Six

As it turned out, my last night in Seattle was also the night of the benefit concert for retired jazz musicians.

Oscar picked us up at seven sharp, and thanks to me, his big red Cadillac sparkled in the evening sunshine.

For the special event, I was wearing one of my mom's old dresses. Grandma had pulled it out of a box in the attic and spent an entire afternoon shortening it and taking in the waist. It was beautiful, made of a rich purple velvet, and I had to admit, as I stared at myself in the mirror, that it looked wonderful. I didn't look too bad, either.

Grandma had pulled out one of her old gowns, fretting and worrying about how out of date and out of style it was, but she refused to spend money to buy anything new. And I'm glad she didn't. It was a slinky, glittery thing that exposed one shoulder and draped to her ankles. It made her look like a movie star.

"You're beautiful, Grandma," was all I could say when she finally glided down the stairs.

"Thank you, Maya. I just hope I can still sing jazz."

"You don't need to worry about that!" I said.

Oscar was waiting for us on the sidewalk, looking like a million dollars in a handsome black tuxedo.

Mr. and Mrs. Richards and Tommy, who Grandma had invited to join us for the evening, met us at the car.

"It's a charity event," Grandma had explained, "for a good cause." I think she was still embarrassed about performing in public after such a long time.

We all crowded into Oscar's Cadillac and headed downtown to Scat's Jazz Club.

As we slowly cruised down the streets, Oscar explained that once upon a time, Seattle, like most cities, had been bustling with music clubs. Over the years, most of them had slowly died away, and only a few, like Scat's, remained. "Before long," he said, with a sad laugh, "they'll end up extinct, just like the dinosaurs."

As we walked inside, Scat's reminded me of an old movie theater, the curtains and carpets faded, the air filled with an accumulation of thirty years of cigarette smoke, old perfume, and cheap wine.

But on this night, Scat's seemed to have come back to life, recapturing a bit of its old glory. The place was packed with people. I recognized many faces from church. But there were a good number of white folks, too. The bar at the back was bustling, and twenty or thirty tables were fanned around an open space on the floor where sat an upright bass, a piano, and drums.

Oscar led us to the best table in the house, right in front. As I slipped into my seat, I noticed a wave from someone in the corner. The lights in the club were low, but not so low that you couldn't recognize people. I smiled at Reverend Gillespie and waved back.

As soon as we were all seated, Oscar strode up to the front and thanked everyone for coming to the show. He reminded people about the purpose of the benefit, that all the money raised would go to the Retired Jazz Musicians' Fund, and that the fund was being administered by Reverend Gillespie's church. He told the crowd that they could also contribute by putting money in the envelopes that were waiting on each table.

That drew a round of applause, interrupted only by Tommy, who yelled out, "PLAY."

I had worried a bit about bringing Tommy along. But no one seemed to mind. In fact, Oscar replied, "Got that right, son. Let's play some music."

A group of black men shuffled out from behind the curtain, taking their places at the instruments. The piano player handed Oscar a saxophone before sitting down at the black and white keys.

The crowd hushed.

From that moment on, I don't remember a lot of the details. What stands out in my mind are the songs. There were some that made me want to cry, and some were so fast and happy that I just couldn't sit still.

Sometime during the evening, Grandma rose to sing. As she stepped into the spotlight, the years seemed to dissolve. I saw her as she must have looked as a young woman. She started with "Lullaby of Birdland," her voice rich and pure, accompanied by Oscar's saxophone and the rest of the band.

About halfway through her song, the oddest thing happened. I've never told anyone about it before, not even Grandma. I blinked my eyes as I saw someone slip out from behind the curtain and take his position in the shadows. He lifted his trombone to his lips and began playing along with the band. I don't know if anyone else could hear him, but I sure could.

It was Billy Bones. My grandfather.

"Play!" I heard Tommy say. I was afraid to glance at him, afraid that whatever dream I was in would vanish.

When he said "Play!" again, I couldn't help myself. I grabbed Tommy's thin wrist and squeezed. That's when I noticed that Tommy was smiling and staring at the same shadowy spot where the ghostly trombone player stood playing.

"Play!" he called again.

I released his wrist and grabbed his hand. *Yes, please play,* I said to myself.

I don't know when Billy Bones slipped away. I would like to think that he winked at me or otherwise acknowledged my presence, but I'm not sure it ever happened. I just know that at some point during one of Grandma's songs, he was gone.

At last, I finally understood the hole that Billy Bones's death had left behind, and not only in the lives of my grandmother, my mom, and all of his friends. His passing had left a huge hole in my life, too—and I was only just beginning to realize it.

It was nearly dawn when Oscar drove us home. The music critic for the local paper had pushed his way forward at the end of the concert, peppering Grandma with all sorts of questions. He wanted to know about an agent, where she was from, and why no one had ever heard of her before.

Oscar intervened, pulling the critic aside before she had to answer. I'm not sure what Oscar told him, but the young man left her alone after that. Her name appeared in the paper a few days later, but it was only a brief mention, not enough to attract too much attention, which is what Oscar knew Grandma would have wanted.

Oscar drove us all home with the top down, despite the chill night air. Everyone was quiet, even Tommy. It was as if we were all afraid that if we said anything, it would break the spell.

By the time we reached home, Tommy was asleep. Mr. Richards carried him into their house. Mrs. Richards gave Grandma a hug and followed them in.

Oscar led us up the steps to the front door. "You sounded even better than in the old days, Ruby," he said.

Grandma gave him a sad smile. "See you next Sunday?"

Oscar's laughter rumbled from his belly. "Maybe so," he said. "Maybe so."

"Good-bye, Mr. Parker," I said.

"Good-bye?"

"I'm going home tomorrow. Remember? Thanks for giving me trombone lessons."

"I hope to see you again sometime," Oscar said gravely. "It has been my distinct pleasure and honor being your teacher . . . "

"And friend?" I said.

"That, too." He kissed me on the hand. "And I'll let you wash my car anytime!" he said, with a laugh.

I waited there until the Cadillac roared back to life, then watched its two yellow beams move down the street, disappearing around the corner and into the night.

"Time for bed, Maya girl," Grandma said. We held hands as we walked up the stairs to her house.

# Chapter Twenty-Seven

I couldn't sleep. Who could, after a night like that?

Wide awake, I kicked off my sheet and lay there for a while, thinking about how I would tell my mom about what had happened, worried about how she'd be when I stepped off the bus, wondering if anything had changed.

A breath of music whispered through the room. The TV next door, I figured. Probably Tommy, awake and discovering the volume knob.

Restless, I crawled out of bed and stood by the window. The Richards' house was dark. I guess even Tommy had to sleep sometimes.

*Did he rock in his sleep?* I wondered. Did he dream? And if he did, what were his dreams like? Were they strange, freaky nightmares or typical ones like mine?

I heard the strains of music again, accompanied by the faint pulse of a bass, and it wasn't coming from outside. It was somewhere in the house.

I listened quietly for a moment more, then padded across the room, opened my door, and peered down the darkened hallway.

Light glowed from beneath Grandma's door. The music was louder now, and I knew exactly where it was coming from.

I hesitated for just a moment, and then I crept silently down the hallway.

I stood there outside her room, listening to that music, unwilling to knock on the door and bother her, but not ready to go back to bed, either.

After a few minutes, I got tired of standing there, so I just lay down in the hallway, my ear near the crack at the bottom of the door. I could hear the music better from there. The floor was hard and cool against my cheek. It felt good.

As the music played, I closed my eyes and listened. I could hear drums, a number of different musical instruments, and more voices than I could identify. Some were high and sweet, like Mom's voice, while others were deeper and richer sounding, sometimes answering the sweet voice, other times going off on their own.

I was still lying there in the silence after the song had ended when Grandma called out: "Best come on in, child. You'll catch your death out there."

How had she known? I scrambled reluctantly to my feet, opened the door, and looked in.

Grandma was sitting on the right side of her bed. She was propped up against a pile of pillows. The room was dark except for a pool of yellow light from the lamp on her nightstand.

"You couldn't sleep, either?"

I shook my head.

"Well then, come on in. I could use some company. This night has wakened memories I thought were long gone and forgotten."

She motioned for me to come to her. I hopped up onto the bed next to her.

"I like that music you're listening to," I said.

"You're a person with taste," Grandma laughed.

That made me giggle. "Sounds like—"

"Jazz," Grandma whispered, stretching the word out so it sounded like the beginning of a poem. "Oh, hush now, here comes the next song. Listen closely, and you'll hear J. J. Johnson playing his trombone. He always reminds me of Billy Bones and the way he sounded when he played."

I snuggled against Grandma's side, closed my eyes, and let the soft notes wash over me.

"I love this," I whispered.

"So do I, honey, so do I."

We listened in silence to a few songs, the sleepy radio announcer mostly keeping quiet, letting the music do the talking.

Grandma suddenly swung her legs over onto the floor. "What's wrong with me?" she exclaimed, her eyes bright. She adjusted her robe. "Come with me."

Barefoot, I followed her up the stairs to the attic.

In the dark at the top, Grandma reached up and found a string. She gave it a jerk, and the bare bulb near the ceiling flared to life.

"Where is it?" she said, scanning the room with tired eyes.

"What are you looking for?" I asked, wanting to help.

But she was already moving, a woman on a mission, so I got out of the way. Grandma ran her hands over hidden objects protected from dust by blankets and sheets.

"Ah, here it is!" she exclaimed, when she at last found the shape she'd been seeking. Dramatically, she pulled back the sheet. "This is my old hi-fi," she proudly announced.

And then she was off again, peering behind boxes. "Now, where are those records?" she muttered under her breath.

"Is this what you want?" I pulled out a box.

"Ah, you found them," she said. "Plug this in over

there." She handed me the end of the cord. "Not sure this old thing even works anymore.

"Now listen to this. This was your grandpa when he played for Stan Wagner's band."

Grandma and I quickly lost track of the hours, listening to the music of Billy Bones and his friends up there in that dusty, dirty, spider-filled attic.

At one point, she pulled out a box full of photo albums. It had pictures of Mom when she was younger. There were older pictures, black-and-white, mostly, of young men and women standing beside fancy old cars, playing music, or having fun at picnics. She pointed out Grandpa and rattled off names I didn't recognize, until she said "Sonny Ray."

"Mr. Johnson?" I interrupted.

Grandma nodded. "We were playing in Kansas City," she said, caressing the glossy surface of the photograph as if she were touching a face.

In between playing the records, which she called 78's, she told me stories about when she and Billy Bones were young. It was like time traveling, only better.

"One time, the car broke down," Grandma said as one song ended, something about the tune having prompted a memory. "Not like that was unusual. Seemed like that car was always just a few miles away from its next breakdown.

This time, it decided to take a break miles away from any-where. There was nobody around but a few old cows, chewing grass near the road.

"We were a few hours outside of Chicago, in farm-land so flat I swear you could stand on the roof of the car and see the Rockies in one direction and the Appalachians in the other.

"Anyway, we pulled the car to a stop on the dusty shoulder and then piled outside to wait for help. Some-times we'd wait a long time. White folks back then weren't much interested in stopping to help a car full of musicians out in the middle of nowhere."

"What about everyone being black?" I asked.

"I suppose that may have had something to do with it, too," Grandma said, with a wink.

"So, Billy Bones gets tired of waiting. He pulls out his case, puts together his trombone, and starts playing to those cows. We all just sat back in the shade of the car and listened.

"Something wonderful came over him that day. He was on fire, playing fast and slow, playing riffs and rhythms, and stringing notes together in ways that at times made us want to weep. At other times, it made us want to jump up and shout.

"He didn't stop until state troopers pulled up in their car and asked us what the hell we were doing.

" 'Just serenading the cows,' Billy said.

"I was afraid the cops were going to arrest him right then and there for his sass, but instead they just laughed. Of course, they didn't bother to lend us a hand. We waited another two hours before a couple of fellows in an old red pickup took pity on us and towed the car to the nearest town."

She told a half dozen more stories like that. We laughed and cried like a couple of good friends instead of a grandmother and her granddaughter.

Finally, I just had to ask her; it was something that had been gnawing at me all summer long.

"What's been wrong?" I blurted out.

"What do you mean?"

"Between you and Mom."

"Ahhh," she sighed. "I wondered when it would be time for that question. It is hard for me to know what your mom thinks."

"I'm not asking what *she* thinks," I interrupted. "I'm asking *you*."

She stared at me for a moment, considering. "Well, it was my fault," she said, finally. "I drove her away. It wasn't my intention." She laughed, a dry humorless cackle. "But I suppose that's the excuse of the scoundrel and the fool."

"I don't understand."

"Is that so?" Grandma said sharply. "I've heard the anger coloring your voice all summer. Not just unhappy with me, but unhappy with your mom. How do you feel now? I notice you haven't gotten around to calling her all summer. Forgiveness can be a hard thing to come by. And how has it been with your daddy gone? Hard on her, I bet. Hard on you, too. Oh, I think you understand."

"Maybe so," I admitted, remembering how I had acted before I left for Seattle, trying every trick and technique I could think of to get Mom to change her mind.

"But I don't want to talk about that, not now," I said. "I want—no, I *need* to know about what happened between you and her. Please!"

She was quiet for a while, her head bowed and her face shadowed. "It's nothing new," she said softly. "It can get hard between a mother and her daughter. You know something about that yourself. In my defense, it wasn't easy raising your mother by myself. I was not the mother she needed or wanted, and I could not be the father she needed or wanted, either. But we made do, both of us. And then one day, I realized she was a grown-up woman. She went out and fell in love with a man I didn't approve of."

"My—"

"Your dad," Grandma finished for me. "I thought she

could do better. Thought they were too young. I told her so. Told him what I thought, too. I knew better than they did. I thought I could make her do the right thing."

I remembered how Grandma had lectured the cab driver that first night in town. I gulped and asked, "What did she do?"

"One morning, she was gone."

"And they got married anyways."

"That, too, though I didn't find out about it until a few months later. I heard nothing more for almost a year, and then I heard from one of her friends that you'd been born. By then, I knew where they lived. I decided to go there. See if we couldn't fix things between us. But it didn't go very well, and after that, well, the months just drifted by, and before long, the months became years."

"So it wasn't 'cause I peed on you," I muttered to myself, unable to hide my relief, happy, almost, to be talking about just about anything other than my mom and dad.

"What was that?"

"My friend Elizabeth. She said you hated us because I probably peed on you when I was a baby."

"That's the most ridiculous thing I've ever heard," Grandma snorted.

"That's what I told her."

"Good for you."

Another piece had been fit into the puzzle of my life. But it didn't make up for the huge piece that was gone: my dad. And nothing ever could.

I hugged my knees tightly, wondering about him.

"I still miss him, you know," Grandma whispered.

"Who?"

"Billy Bones. I've missed him every single day since he was gone."

"My dad, too," I whispered.

I felt my grandma touch my hair, her way of letting me know that I was not alone. I was glad she didn't ruin it all by saying she knew how I felt.

"Does it ever get any better?" I said.

When she didn't reply, I looked up. She was crying, her face streaked with tears. She wiped her eyes and shrugged, and that's when I realized I was wrong. She did know how I felt. Not exactly, but close enough.

"I suppose I got used to it, child," she said, "but I never got over it."

"I don't understand."

"You love your daddy." It was a statement, not a question. And now it was my turn to cry.

"Of course you love him. I loved my Billy, too. Still do. Getting over that would mean it never mattered."

"But it hurts," I said.

"Yes, it does. And when it gets too bad, you have your mom, and Elizabeth, and your other friends to help."

"And you?"

Grandma smiled and touched my hair again. "I'm not going away, not ever."

We were both quiet for a while. "What's going to happen when I get back home?" I asked, breaking the silence.

"What do you want to happen?"

"I don't want it to end," I snapped, my voice rising. "I feel, I feel—"

"Feel what?"

"Like I just found you," I shouted. "And I don't want to give you up and have it like it was before, not even knowing you."

Grandma smiled. "I feel the same way, honey," she said.

"So, what are you and Mom going to do about it?" I asked, putting my hands on my hips.

"We'll have to see where it goes. But your mom and I have exchanged letters."

"Letters? Are you writing about me?"

"Of course," Grandma said. "And other things, as well. Satisfied?"

Now it was my turn to smile.

"Good, then. I'm tired of talking."

Without even asking, she put on some more music, closed her eyes, and leaned back against the sheet-covered attic chair.

# Chapter Twenty-Eight

I suppose the weather was perfect for my last day in Seattle—gray and rainy.

I waited at the curb, holding hands with Sonny Ray, while Grandma pulled the front door closed and joined us. It was still a week before Labor Day, but I could smell the earthy hint of autumn in the air. It made me sad. Another change was coming.

Sonny Ray gave me an affectionate hug just before I climbed into the taxi. "Be safe, missy," he whispered.

"You too." I choked back tears.

I was glad he was going to be renting the spare room in the basement from Grandma. It made me feel better knowing she wouldn't be all alone after I was gone.

I had said my other good-byes earlier. It had taken me a while to find Harry S. Truman. He was in the backyard, all stretched out beneath a rhododendron bush long past its bloom. I pulled him onto my lap, scratched his head and beneath his chin, and when he finally decided to give up and start purring, I kissed him on the nose. "Take good care of yourself, Mr. President," I said.

Then, at the Richards' house, Mr. Richards shook my hand formally, thanking me for being Tommy's friend. Mrs. Richards just cried, hugging me tight and asking me to please write.

Before I left their house, I stood and watched Tommy from the doorway to his room for a moment. He was sitting on the floor, rocking back and forth, occupied by a world and thoughts I still could only imagine. I wondered if he knew what was going on, that I was about to leave him.

"Bye, Mr. Jazz-Man Tommy," I had said, brushing his mop of brown hair lightly with the back of my hand, not minding that he didn't even look at me. "Write me some Seattle blues someday," I whispered.

As I settled into the back seat of the cab, I noticed that Tommy was watching from the upstairs window. Unlike earlier, he was looking right at me.

I raised my hand in a wave and mouthed good-bye, surprised that I suddenly felt like crying. I suppose I hadn't realized until that instant just how deeply he had snuck into my heart.

Tommy raised his hand, too, and I could see him

mouthing something behind the glass. Of course, it wasn't *good-bye*, or *see ya later*, or anything like that. It took me a moment, and then I realized what he was saying: "Play."

Then his gaze crumbled. He began to rock. I wondered if I would ever see him again.

At the bus station, Grandma gave me a final kiss and then tucked a brown paper bag containing my lunch under my arm.

"Oops, almost forgot," she said. She reached behind a stack of luggage and pulled out that long, brown case covered with worn stickers from faraway places like Miami Beach, Scranton, and Paris.

"I've had this forgotten and hidden long enough," she said softly.

Playing Grandpa's trombone all summer was one thing, but having it for my very own was something else entirely.

"I can't," I stuttered. "It's too, too—"

"Oh, hush now," Grandma said, with a laugh. "Don't you think Billy Bones would want you to have it? Of course he would! The last thing he would have wanted was this ol' trombone lying around and forgotten forever in the attic. It was made for making music—just like you were."

I grabbed the handle, hugging the case close to my chest. "Someday—" I whispered.

"What was that, honey?"

"Someday you're going to hear me playing on the radio," I blurted out. "Just like last night."

"Is that a promise?"

"Cross my heart," I said solemnly.

She kissed me on the top of my head and then pushed me up the steps onto the bus.

I settled into the vacant seat behind the bus driver, still stunned by Grandma's gift.

"How was your summer?" he asked.

"Gus!" I exclaimed.

"The one and only," Gus said, tipping his hat. "What have you got there?"

"It's my grandfather's trombone. And now it's mine," I replied, with joy.

"Maybe you can play me something once we get out on the road," said Gus.

"What about everybody else?" I questioned, jabbing a thumb in the direction of the passengers behind me.

"It's my ship," Gus said, "and what this captain says, goes."

Gus reached forward and pulled the door closed. I pressed my face against the glass, watching Grandma standing there next to the bus. I realized once again how much she looked like my mom. I saw it in her face and in the proud way she held her head.

The bus started with a grumble and roar. Grandma began to wave. I saw her mouth move. It took me a moment before I realized what she was saying: "I love you."

"Stop!" I screamed. "I forgot to tell my grandma something important."

Gus looked up in the mirror, started shaking his head, and then he saw my face. He jammed on the brakes, then pulled the lever and opened the door. "Be quick" was all he said.

I bounced down the stairs and dashed around the front of the bus.

"Grandma," I shouted, running up to her and locking my arms around her waist. "I almost forgot," I said breathlessly.

"My goodness! What is it, dear?"

"I was just wondering if I could, well, come back again someday?"

Grandma's lip began to tremble. When I looked up into her beautiful face, there were tears in her eyes. Her mouth was working as she tried to find the words.

"Yes, of course," she said finally, softly. "I'd love to have you stay with me again. It would mean the world to me."

I almost didn't say the rest of what was on my mind. Maybe it was better not to push my luck. But when had I ever been one to hold back? I decided to shoot for the moon.

"I want to bring Mom with me when I come back."

This time, she didn't say a word. She simply couldn't. She finally gave up and just smiled, big and bright, and then she nodded. "Good!" was all she could manage.

"Okay," I said, releasing her from my grasp and giving her one of my very special smiles.

"What is it?" Grandma asked, finding the rest of her voice. "I know what that look means. It's just like the cat that ate the canary."

"Well," I said, kicking at the small pebbles on the ground. I wasn't ready to admit anything just yet. I had planned to write Grandma a letter when I got home. But since she'd asked, I plunged in.

"I've already talked to Mom. Last night, when she called. We're going to come up for Thanksgiving—"

She didn't give me a chance to finish. She gathered me up in her arms and then began to laugh.

"Just inviting yourself up, I see," she said. "Was that your idea?"

I nodded.

"Well, you tell Jenny that I'd love to have you both come up for Thanksgiving—and any other time you'd like to visit."

"You should tell her yourself, Grandma," I suggested.

"I think I'll do just that."

Michael Wenberg

# Author's Note

As Maya eventually learns, Tommy Richards has a serious disorder called autism. Among other things, autism hinders the development of a person's ability to interact with other people. However, like Tommy, some people who have this disorder exhibit extraordinary abilities. One example is the jazz pianist Matt Savage. You can learn more about him at his Web site, www.savagerecords.com.

There are also a number of sites online where you can find more information about autism. Here are three good ones: the Autism Collaboration (www.autism.org), the Autism and PDD Support Network (www.autism-pdd.net), and the Autism Society of America (www.autism-society.org).

The trombone has an interesting legacy and a versatility that gives it a place in rock bands, jazz combos, salsa bands, or symphony orchestras. For more information about the trombone and trombone playing, check with a music teacher at your local school, or visit the Web sites of the Online Trombone Journal (www.trombone.org) or the International Trombone Association (www.ita-web.org).

Better yet, find an old trombone in an attic or somewhere else and start blowing.

The history of American jazz is peppered with many wonderful trombone players. One of them is Melba Liston. She played trombone at a time when jazz bands—with rare exceptions—were all-male groups. Women were routinely discouraged from becoming members—unless they were singers, of course. In addition to playing with Dizzy Gillespie and many other jazz headliners, Liston ventured into music composition and arranging. Later in her career, she collaborated with pianist Randy Weston on several albums. A number of Web sites have more information about Melba Liston. National Public Radio's Web site is a good place to start. Go to www.npr.org, and search for "Melba Liston."

If you're curious about jazz and blues and want to learn more, here are three great Web sites you can visit to get started: www.pbs.org/jazz, www.pbs.org/theblues, and www.jazz-inamerica.org

But of course, the best way to learn about jazz or blues is to listen to them.